"This great girl my child? Really it's enough to make a man feel old," he said.

Elsie Dinsmore

By

MARTHA FINLEY

Illustrated by

HENRY MUHEIM

THE
SAALFIELD PUBLISHING COMPANY
Akron, Ohio   New York

Chapter 1

I never saw an eye so bright,
 And yet so soft as hers;
It sometimes swam in liquid light,
 And sometimes swam in tears;
It seemed a beauty set apart
 For softness and for sighs.
—Mrs. Welby

THE schoolroom at Roselands was a very
pleasant apartment; the ceiling, it is true, was
somewhat lower than in the more modern por-
tion of the building, but the effect was relieved by windows reaching from floor to
ceiling, and opening on a veranda which over-
looked a lovely flower garden, beyond which
were fields and woods and hills. The view
from the veranda was very beautiful, and the
room itself looked most inviting, with its neat
matting, its windows draped with snow-white
muslin, its comfortable chairs, and pretty
rosewood desks.

Within this pleasant apartment sat Miss
Day with her pupils, six in number. She was
giving a lesson to Enna, the youngest, the
spoiled darling of the family, the pet and play-

thing of both father and mother. It was always a trying task to both teacher and scholar, for Enna was very wilful, and her teacher's patience by no means inexhaustible.

"There!" exclaimed Miss Day, shutting the book and giving it an impatient toss onto the desk, "go, for I might as well try to teach old Bruno."

And Enna walked away with a pout on her pretty face.

"Young ladies and gentlemen," said Miss Day, looking at her watch, "I shall leave you to your studies for an hour, at the end of which time I shall return to hear your recitations, when those who have attended properly to their duties will be permitted to ride out with me to visit the fair."

"Oh! that will be jolly!" exclaimed Arthur, a bright-eyed, mischief-loving boy of ten.

"Hush!" said Miss Day, sternly, "let me hear no more such exclamations; and remember that you will not go unless your lessons are thoroughly learned. Louise and Lora," addressing two young girls of the respective ages of twelve and fourteen, "that French exercise must be perfect, and your English lessons as well. Elsie," to a little girl of eight, sitting alone at a desk near one of the windows, and bending over a slate with an appearance of great industry, "every figure of that example must be correct, your geography lesson recited perfectly, and a page in your copybook written without a blot."

"Yes, ma'am," said the child meekly, raising a pair of large, soft eyes of the darkest hazel for an instant to her teacher's face.

"And see that none of you leave the room until I return," continued the governess. "Walter, if you miss one word of that spelling, you will have to stay at home and learn it over."

"Unless mamma interferes, as she will be pretty sure to do," muttered Arthur, as the door closed on Miss Day.

For about ten minutes after her departure all was quiet in the schoolroom, each seemingly completely absorbed in study. But at the end of that time Arthur sprang up, and flinging his book across the room exclaimed, "There! I know my lesson; and if I didn't, I shouldn't study another bit for old Day, or Night either."

"Do be quiet, Arthur," said his sister Louise, "I can't study in such a racket."

Arthur stole on tiptoe across the room, and coming up behind Elsie, tickled the back of her neck with a feather.

She started, saying in a pleading tone, "Please, Arthur, don't."

"It pleases me to do," he said, repeating the experiment.

Elsie changed her position, saying in the same gentle, persuasive tone, "O Arthur! *please* let me alone, or I never shall be able to do this example."

"What! all this time on one example! Why, I could have done it half a dozen times over."

"I have been over and over it," replied the little girl in a tone of despondency, "and still there are two figures that just will not come right."

"How do you know they are not right, little puss?" shaking her curls as he spoke.

"Oh! please, Arthur, don't pull my hair. I have the answer—that's the way I know."

"Well, then, why don't you just set the figures down? I would."

"Oh! no, indeed; that would not be honest."

"Pooh! nonsense! nobody would be the wiser, nor the poorer."

"No, but it would be just like telling a lie. But I can never get it right while you are bothering me so," said Elsie, laying her slate aside in despair. Then taking out her geography, she began studying most diligently. But Arthur continued his persecutions—tickling her, pulling her hair, twitching the book out of her hand, and talking almost incessantly, making remarks, and asking questions till at last Elsie said, as if just ready to cry, "Indeed, Arthur, if you don't let me alone, I shall never be able to get my lessons."

"Go away then; take your book out on the veranda, and learn your lessons there," said Louise. "I'll call you when Miss Day comes."

"Oh! no, Louise, I cannot do that, because it would be disobedience," replied Elsie, taking out her writing materials.

Arthur stood over her criticising every letter she made, and finally jogged her elbow in such a way as to cause her to drop all the ink in her pen upon the paper, making quite a large blot.

"Oh!" cried the little girl, bursting into

tears, "now I shall lose my ride, for Miss Day will not let me go."

Arthur, who was really not very vicious, felt some compunction when he saw the mischief he had done. "Never mind, Elsie," said he, "I can fix it yet. Just let me tear out this page, and you can begin again on the next, and I'll not bother you. I'll make these two figures come right, too," he added.

"Thank you, Arthur," said the little girl, smiling through her tears, "but it would not be honest to do either, and I had rather stay at home than be deceitful."

"Very well, miss," said he, tossing his head and walking away, "since you won't let me help you, it is all your own fault if you have to stay at home."

"Elsie," exclaimed Louise, "I have no patience with you! such ridiculous scruples as you are always raising. I shall not pity you one bit if you are obliged to stay at home."

Elsie made no reply, but, brushing away a tear, bent over her writing, taking great pains with every letter, though saying sadly to herself all the time, "It's of no use, for that great ugly blot will spoil it all."

She finished her page, and, excepting the unfortunate blot, it all looked very neat indeed, showing plainly that it had been written with great care. She then took up her slate and patiently went over and over every figure of the troublesome example, trying to discover where her mistake had been. But before the two troublesome figures had been made right, the hour was past, and Miss Day returned.

"Oh!" thought Elsie, "if she will only hear the others first, I may be able to get this and the geography ready yet; and perhaps, if Arthur will be generous enough to tell her about the blot, she may excuse me for it."

But it was a vain hope. Miss Day had no sooner seated herself at her desk than she called, "Elsie, come here and say that lesson; and bring your copybook and slate, that I may examine your work."

Elsie tremblingly obeyed.

The lesson, though a difficult one, was very tolerably recited, but Miss Day handed back the book with a frown, saying, "I told you the recitation must be perfect, and it was not."

She was always more severe with Elsie than with any other of her pupils.

"There are two incorrect figures in this example," said she, laying down the slate, after glancing over its contents. Then taking up the copybook, she exclaimed, "Careless, disobedient child! did I not caution you to be careful not to blot your book! There will be no ride for you this morning. You have failed in everything. Go to your seat. Make that example right, and do the next; learn your geography lesson over, and write another page in your copybook; and, mind, if there is a blot on it, you will get no dinner."

During this scene Arthur stood at his desk pretending to study, but glancing every now and then at Elsie, with a conscience evidently ill at ease. She cast an imploring glance at him, as she returned to her seat; but he turned away his head, muttering, "It's all her own fault, for she wouldn't let me help her."

As he looked up again, he caught his sister Lora's eyes fixed on him with an expression of scorn and contempt. He colored violently, and dropped his eyes upon his book.

"Miss Day," said Lora, indignantly, "I see Arthur does not mean to speak, and as I cannot bear to see such injustice, I must tell you that it is all his fault that Elsie has failed in her lessons; for she tried her very best, but he teased her incessantly, and also jogged her elbow and made her spill the ink on her book; and to her credit she was too honorable to tear out the leaf from her copybook or to let him make her example right; both of which he very generously proposed doing after causing all the mischief."

"Is this so, Arthur?" asked Miss Day.

The boy hung his head, but made no reply.

"Very well, then," said Miss Day, "you too must stay at home."

"Surely," said Lora, in surprise, "you will not keep Elsie, since I have shown you that she was not to blame."

"Miss Lora," replied her teacher haughtily, "I wish you to understand that I am not to be dictated to by my pupils."

Lora bit her lip, but said nothing, and Miss Day went on hearing the lessons without fur- ther remark.

In the meantime Elsie sat at her desk, striv- ing to conquer the feelings of anger and in- dignation that were swelling in her breast; for Elsie often had a fierce contest with her naturally quick temper. Yet it was seldom, very seldom, that word or tone or look betrayed the existence of such feelings; and it was a common remark in the family that Elsie had no spirit.

The recitations were scarcely finished when the door opened and a lady entered dressed for a ride.

"Not through yet, Miss Day?" she asked.

"Yes, madam, we are just done," replied the teacher.

"Well, I hope your pupils have all done their duty this morning, and are ready to accompany us to the fair," said Mrs. Dinsmore. "But what is the matter with Elsie?"

"She has failed in all her exercises, and therefore has been told that she must remain at home," replied Miss Day, with heightened color and in a tone of anger, "and as Miss Lora tells me that Master Arthur was partly the cause, I have forbidden him also to accompany us."

"Excuse me, Miss Day, for correcting you," said Lora, a little indignantly, "but I did not say *partly*. It was *entirely* his fault."

"Hush, hush, Lora," said her mother, a little

impatiently, "how can you be sure of any such thing?   Miss Day, I must beg of you to excuse Arthur this once, for I have quite set my heart on taking him along.   He is fond of mischief, I know, but he is only a child, and you must not be too hard upon him."

"Very well, madam," replied the governess stiffly, "you have of course the best right to control your own children."

Mrs. Dinsmore turned to leave the room.

"Mamma," asked Lora, "is not Elsie to be allowed to go, too?"

"Elsie is not my child, and I have nothing to say about it.   Miss Day is much better able than I to judge whether or no she is deserving of punishment," replied Mrs. Dinsmore, sailing out of the room.

"You will let her go, Miss Day?" said Lora inquiringly.

"Miss Lora," replied Miss Day angrily, "I have already told you I was not to be dictated to.   I have said Elsie must remain at home, and I shall not break my word."

"Such injustice!" muttered Lora.

"Lora," said Louise, impatiently, "why need you concern yourself with Elsie's affairs?   For my part, I have no pity for her, so full as she is of nonsensical scruples."

Miss Day crossed the room to where Elsie was sitting leaning her head upon the desk, struggling hard to keep down the feelings of anger and indignation aroused by the unjust treatment she had received.

"Did I not order you to learn that lesson over?" said the governess, "and why are you sitting here idling?"

Elsie dared not speak lest her anger should show itself in words; so merely raised her head, and hastily brushing away her tears, opened the book. But Miss Day seemed determined to vent her displeasure upon her victim.

"Why do you not speak?" she exclaimed, seizing Elsie by the arm and shaking her violently. "Answer me this instant! Why have you been idling all the morning?"

"I have *not*," replied the child hastily, stung to the quick by her unjust violence. "I have tried hard to do my duty, and you are punishing me when I don't deserve it at all."

"How dare you? There! take that for your impertinence," said Miss Day, giving her a box on the ear.

Elsie was about to make a still more angry reply; but she restrained herself, and turning to her book, tried to study, though the hot, blinding tears came so thick and fast that she could not see a letter.

"De carriage am waiting, ladies, an' missus in a hurry," said a servant, opening the door; and Miss Day hastily quitted the room, followed by Louise and Lora; and Elsie was left alone.

She laid down the geography, and opening her desk, took out a small pocket Bible, which bore the marks of frequent use. She turned over the leaves as though seeking for some particular passage; at length she found it, and wiping away the blinding tears, she read, "For this is thankworthy, if a man for conscience toward God endure grief, suffering wrongfully. For what glory is it if, when ye be buffeted for your faults, ye shall take it patiently? but if when ye do well, and suffer for it, ye take it patiently, this is acceptable with God. For even hereunto were ye called; because Christ also suffered for us, leaving us an example that ye should follow His steps."

"Oh! I have not done it. I did not take it

patiently. I am afraid I am not following in His steps," she cried, bursting into an agony of tears and sobs.

"My dear little girl, what is the matter?" asked a kind voice, and a soft hand was gently laid on her shoulder.

The child looked up hastily. "O Miss Allison!" she said, "is it you? I thought I was quite alone."

"And so you were, my dear, until this moment," replied the lady, drawing up a chair and sitting down close beside her. "I was on the veranda, and hearing sobs, came in to see if I could be of any assistance. You look very much distressed. Will you not tell me the cause of your sorrow?"

Elsie answered only by a fresh burst of tears.

"They have all gone to the fair and left you at home alone; perhaps to learn a lesson you have failed in reciting?" said the lady, inquiringly.

"Yes, ma'am," said the child, "but that is not the worst"; and her tears fell faster, as she laid the little Bible on the desk, and pointed with her finger to the words she had been reading. "Oh!" she sobbed, "I—I did not do it; I did not bear it patiently. I was treated unjustly, and punished when I was not to blame, and I grew angry. Oh! I'm afraid I shall never be like Jesus! never, never."

The child's distress seemed very great, and Miss Allison was extremely surprised. She was a visitor who had been in the house only a few days, and, herself a devoted Christian, had been greatly pained by the utter disregard of the family in which she was sojourning for the teachings of God's word. Rose Allison was from the North, and Mr. Dinsmore, the proprietor of Roselands, was an old friend of her father, to whom he had been paying a visit, and finding Rose in delicate health, he had prevailed upon her parents to allow her to spend the winter months with his family in the more congenial clime of their Southern home.

"My poor child," she said, passing her arm around the little one's waist, "my poor little Elsie! that is your name, is it not?"

"Yes, ma'am; Elsie Dinsmore."

"Dear Elsie, 'if we confess our sins, He is faithful and just to forgive us.' "

"Yes, ma'am," said the child; "I have asked

Him to forgive me, and I know He has; but I am so sorry, oh! so sorry that I have grieved and displeased Him; for, O Miss Allison! I do love Jesus, and want to be like Him always."

"I am very, very glad to learn that you love Jesus, and are striving to do His will. I love Him too, and we will love one another; for you know He says, 'By this shall men know that ye are my disciples, if ye have love one to another,'" said Miss Allison, stroking the little girl's hair and kissing her tenderly.

"Will you love me? Oh! how glad I am!" exclaimed the child joyfully. "I have nobody to love me but poor old mammy."

"And who is mammy?" asked the lady.

"My dear old nurse, who has always taken care of me. Have you not seen her, ma'am?"

"Perhaps I may. I have seen a number of nice old colored women about here since I came. But, Elsie, will you tell me who taught you about Jesus?"

"It was dear old mammy who first told me how He suffered and died on the cross for us," replied the little girl earnestly. Her eyes filled with tears and her voice quivered with emotion. "She used to talk to me about it just as soon as I could understand anything," she continued, "and then she would tell me that my own dear mamma loved Jesus, and had gone to be with Him in heaven; and how, when she was dying, she put me—a little, wee baby, I was then not quite a week old—into her arms, and said, 'Mammy, take my dear little baby and love her, and take care of her just as you did of me; and O mammy! be sure that you teach her to love God.' Would you like to see my mamma, Miss Allison?"

And as she spoke she drew from her bosom a miniature set in gold and diamonds, which she wore suspended by a gold chain around her neck, and put it in Rose's hand.

It was the likeness of a young girl, not more than fifteen or sixteen years of age. She was very beautiful, with a sweet, gentle, winning countenance, the same soft hazel eyes and golden-brown curls that the little Elsie possessed; the same regular features, pure complexion, and sweet smile.

Miss Allison gazed at it a moment in silent admiration; then, turning from it to the child with a puzzled expression, she said: "But, Elsie, I do not understand; are you not sister to Enna and the rest, and is not Mrs. Dinsmore own mother to them all?"

"Yes, ma'am, to all of them, but not to me or my papa. Their brother Horace is my papa, and so they are all my aunts and uncles."

"Indeed," said the lady, musingly, "I thought you looked very unlike the rest. And your papa is away, is he not, Elsie?"

"Yes, ma'am; he is in Europe. He has been away almost ever since I was born, and I have never seen him. Oh, how I do wish he would come home! how I long to see him! Do you think he would love me, Miss Allison? Do you think he would take me on his knee and pet me, as grandpa does Enna?"

"I should think he would, dear; I don't know how he could help loving his own dear little girl," said the lady, again kissing the little rosy cheek. "But now," she added, rising, "I must go away and let you learn your lesson."

Then taking up the little Bible and turning over the leaves, she asked: "Would you like to come to my room sometimes in the mornings and evenings and read this book with me, Elsie?"

"Oh! yes, ma'am, dearly!" exclaimed the child, her eyes sparkling with pleasure.

"Come then this evening, if you like; and now good-bye for the present." And pressing another kiss on the child's cheek, she left her and went back to her own room, where she found her friend Adelaide Dinsmore, a young lady near her own age, and the eldest daughter of the family. Adelaide was seated on a sofa, busily employed with some fancywork.

"You see, I am making myself quite at home," she said, looking up as Rose entered. "I cannot imagine where you have been all this time."

"Can you not? In the schoolroom, talking with little Elsie. Do you know, Adelaide, I thought she was your sister, but she tells me not."

"No, she is Horace's child. I supposed you knew; but if you do not, I may just as well tell you the whole story. Horace was a very wild boy, petted and spoiled, and always used to having his own way; and when he was about seventeen—quite a forward youth he was, too —he must needs go to New Orleans to spend some months with a schoolmate; and there he met, and fell desperately in love with, a very beautiful girl a year or two younger than himself, an orphan and very wealthy. Fearing that objections would be made on the score of their youth, he persuaded her to consent to a private marriage, and they had been man and wife for some months before either her friends or his suspected it.

"Well, when it came at last to papa's ears, he was very angry, both on account of their extreme youth and because, as Elsie Grayson's father had made all his money by trade, he did not consider her quite my brother's equal; so he called Horace home and sent him North to college. Then he studied law, and since that he has been traveling in foreign lands. But to return to his wife. It seems that her guardian was quite as much opposed to the match as papa, and the poor girl was made to believe that she should never see her husband again. All their letters were intercepted, and finally she was told that he was dead; so, as Aunt Chloe says, 'she grew thin and pale, and weak and melancholy,' and while the little Elsie was not quite a week old, she died. We never saw her; she died in her guardian's house, and

*Little Elsie stayed in charge of Aunt Chloe,
who had nursed her mother before her.*

there the little Elsie stayed in charge of Aunt Chloe, who was an old servant in the family and had nursed her mother before her, and of the housekeeper, Mrs. Murray, a pious old Scotch woman, until about four years ago, when her guardian's death broke up the family, and then they came to us. Horace never comes home, and does not seem to care for his child, for he never mentions her in his letters, except when it is necessary in the way of business."

"She is a dear little thing," said Rose. "I am sure he could not help loving her, if he could only see her."

"Oh! yes, she is well enough, and I often feel sorry for the lonely little thing, but the truth is, I believe we are a little jealous of her; she is so extremely beautiful, and heiress to such an immense fortune. Mamma often frets and says that one of these days Elsie will quite eclipse her younger daughters."

"But then," said Rose, "she is almost as near—her own granddaughter."

"No, she is not so very near," replied Adelaide, "for Horace is not mamma's son. He was seven or eight years old when she married papa, and I think she was never particularly fond of him."

"Ah! yes," thought Rose, "that explains it. Poor little Elsie! No wonder you pine for your father's love and grieve over the loss of the mother you never knew!"

Chapter 2

When forced to part from those we love,
  Though sure to meet tomorrow,
We yet a kind of anguish prove
  And feel a touch of sorrow.
But oh! what words can paint the fears
  When from these friends we sever,
Perhaps to part for months—for years—
  Perhaps to part forever.

—ANONYMOUS

WHEN Miss Allison had gone, and Elsie found herself once more quite alone, she set to work diligently at her studies, and before the party returned was quite prepared to meet Miss Day, having attended faithfully to all she had required of her. The lesson was recited without the smallest mistake, every figure of the examples worked out correctly, and the page of the copybook neatly and carefully written.

Miss Day had been in a very captious mood all day, and seemed really provoked that Elsie had not given her the smallest excuse for fault-finding. Handing the book back to her, she said, very coldly, "I see you can do your duties well enough when you choose."

Elsie felt keenly the injustice of the remark

32

and longed to say that she had tried quite as earnestly in the morning; but she resolutely crushed down the indignant feeling, and calling to mind the rash words that had cost her so many repentant tears, she replied meekly, "I am sorry I did not succeed better this morning, Miss Day, though I did really try; and I am still more sorry for the saucy answer I gave you; and I ask your pardon for it."

"You *ought* to be sorry," replied Miss Day, severely, "and I hope you are; for it was a very impertinent speech indeed, and deserving of a much more severe punishment than you received. Now go, and never let me hear anything of the kind from you again."

Poor little Elsie's eyes filled with tears at these ungracious words, accompanied by a still more ungracious manner; but she turned away without a word, and placing her books and slate carefully in her desk, left the room.

Rose Allison was sitting alone in her room that evening, thinking of her far-distant home, when hearing a gentle rap at her door, she rose and opened it to find Elsie standing there with her Bible in her hand.

"Come in, darling," she said, stooping to

give the little one a kiss, "I am very glad to see you."

"I may stay with you for half an hour, Miss Allison, if you like," said the child, seating herself on the low ottoman pointed out by Rose, "and then mammy is coming to put me to bed."

"It will be a very pleasant half hour to both of us, I hope," replied Rose.

They read a chapter together—Rose now and then pausing to make a few explanations—and then kneeling down, she offered up a prayer for the teachings of the Spirit, and for God's blessing on themselves and all their dear ones.

"Dear little Elsie," she said, folding the child in her arms, when they had risen from their knees, "how I love you already, and how very glad I am to find that there is one in this house beside myself who loves Jesus."

"Yes, dear Miss Allison; and there is *more* than one, for mammy loves Him, too, very dearly," replied the little girl earnestly.

"Does she, darling? Then I must love her, too, for I cannot help loving all who love my Saviour."

"That is mammy coming for me," said Elsie, as a low knock was heard at the door.

"Come in," said Rose, and the door opened, and a very nice colored woman of middle age, looking beautifully neat in her snow-white apron and turban, entered with a low courtesy, asking, "Is my little missus ready for bed?"

"Yes," said Elsie, jumping off Rose's lap, "but come here, mammy; I want to introduce you to Miss Allison."

"How do you do, Aunt Chloe? I am very glad to know you, since Elsie tells me you are a servant of the same blessed Master whom I love and try to serve," said Rose.

" 'Deed I hope I is, missus," replied Chloe, "I'se only a poor old black sinner, but de good Lord Jesus, He loves me jes' de same as if I was white, an' I love Him an' all His chillen with all my heart. But good-night, missus; I must put my chile to bed," she added, taking Elsie's hand.

"Good-night, Aunt Chloe; come in again," said Rose. "And good-night to you, too, dear little Elsie," folding the little girl again in her arms.

"Ain't dat a bressed young lady, darlin'?"

exclaimed Chloe, earnestly, as she prepared her young charge for bed.

"O mammy, I love her so much! she's so good and kind," replied the child.

"She reminds me of your dear mamma, Miss Elsie, but she's not so handsome," replied the nurse with a tear in her eye, "ole Chloe tinks dere's nebber any lady so beautiful as her dear young missus was."

Elsie drew out the miniature and kissed it, murmuring, "Dear, darling mamma!" then put it back in her bosom again, for she always wore it day and night. She was standing in her white nightdress, the tiny white feet just peeping from under it, while Chloe brushed back her curls.

"Dere now, darlin', you's ready for bed," she exclaimed, giving the child a hug and a kiss.

"No, mammy, not quite," replied the little girl, and gliding away to the side of the bed, she knelt down and offered up her evening prayer.

Miss Allison spent the whole fall and winter at Roselands; and it was very seldom during all that time that she and Elsie failed to have their morning and evening reading and prayer together. Rose became strongly attached to her, and the little girl fully returned her affection.

Elsie was very sensitive and affectionate, and felt keenly the want of sympathy and love, for which, at the time of Rose's coming, she had no one to look to but poor old Chloe, who loved her with all her heart.

It is true, Adelaide sometimes treated her almost affectionately, and Lora, who had a very strong sense of justice, occasionally interfered and took her part when she was very unjustly accused, but no one seemed really to care for her, and she often felt sad and lonely. Mr. Dinsmore, though her own grandfather, treated her with entire neglect, seemed to have not the slightest affection for her, and usually spoke of her as "old Grayson's grandchild." Mrs. Dinsmore really disliked her, because she looked upon her as the child of a stepson for whom she had never felt any affection, and also as the future rival of her own children.

Elsie talked much and thought more of her absent and unknown father and longed with

an intensity of desire for his return home. It
was her dream, by day and by night, that he
had come, that he had taken her to his heart,
calling her "his own darling child, his precious
little Elsie," for such were the loving epithets
she often heard lavished upon Enna, and which
she longed to hear addressed to herself. But
from month to month and year to year that
longed-for return had been delayed until the
little heart had grown sick with hope deferred,
and was often weary with its almost hopeless
waiting.

And so the winter glided away, and spring
came, and Miss Allison must soon return home.
It was now the last day of March, and her
departure had been fixed for the second of
April. For a number of weeks Elsie had been
engaged, during all her spare moments, in
knitting a purse for Rose, wishing to give her
something which was the work of her own
hands, knowing that as such it would be more
prized by her friend than a costlier gift. She
had just returned from her afternoon ride, and
taking out her work, she sat down to finish it.
She was in her own room with no companion
but Chloe, who sat knitting beside her as usual.

Elsie worked on silently for some time, then suddenly holding up her purse, she exclaimed: "See, mammy, it is all done but putting on the tassel! Isn't it pretty? And won't dear Miss Allison be pleased with it?"

It really was very pretty indeed, of crimson and gold, and beautifully knit, and Chloe, looking at it with admiring eyes, said, "I spec she will, darlin'. I tink it's bery handsome."

At this moment Enna opened the door and came in.

Elsie hastily attempted to conceal the purse by thrusting it into her pocket, but it was too late, for Enna had seen it, and running toward her, cried out, "Now, Elsie, just give that to me!"

"No, Enna," replied Elsie, mildly, "I cannot let you have it, because it is for Miss Rose."

"I will have it," exclaimed the child, resolutely, "and if you don't give it to me at once I shall just go and tell mamma."

"I will let you take it in your hand a few moments to look at it, if you will be careful not to soil it, Enna," said Elsie, in the same gentle tone, "and if you wish, I will get some more silk and beads and make you one just like it; but I cannot give you this, because I would not have time to make another for Miss Rose."

"No, I shall just have that one; and I shall have it to keep," said Enna, attempting to snatch it out of Elsie's hand.

But Elsie held it up out of her reach, and, after trying several times in vain to get it, Enna left the room, crying and screaming with passion.

Chloe locked the door, saying, "Great pity, darlin', we forgot to do dat 'fore Miss Enna came. I'se 'fraid she gwine bring missus for make you gib um up."

Elsie sat down to her work again, but she was very pale, and her little hands trembled with agitation, and her eyes were full of tears.

Chloe's fears were but too well founded; for the next moment hasty steps were heard in the passage, and the handle of the door was laid hold of with no very gentle grasp; and then, as it refused to yield to her touch, Mrs. Dinsmore's voice was heard in an angry tone commanding, "Open this door instantly."

Chloe looked at her young mistress.

"You will have to," said Elsie tearfully, slipping her work into her pocket again, and lifting up her heart in prayer for patience and meekness, for she well knew she would have need of both.

Mrs. Dinsmore entered, leading the sobbing Enna by the hand; her face was flushed with passion, and addressing Elsie in tones of violent anger, she asked, "What is the meaning of all this, you good-for-nothing hussy? Why are you always tormenting this poor child? Where is that paltry trifle that all this fuss is about? Let me see it this instant."

Elsie drew the purse from her pocket, saying in tearful, trembling tones, "It is a purse I was making for Miss Rose, ma'am; and I offered to make another just like it for Enna; but I cannot give her this one, because there would not be time to make another before Miss Rose goes away."

"You *can* not give it to her, indeed! You *will* not, you mean; but I say you *shall;* and I'll see if I'm not mistress in my own house. Give it to the child this instant; I'll not have her crying her eyes out that you may be humored in all your whims. There are plenty of handsomer ones to be had in the city, and if you are too mean to make her a present of it, I'll buy you another to-morrow."

"But that would not be my work, and this is," replied Elsie, still retaining the purse, loath to let it go.

"Nonsense! What difference will that make to Miss Rose?" said Mrs. Dinsmore; and snatching it out of her hand, she gave it to Enna, saying, "There, my pet, you shall have it. Elsie is a naughty, mean, stingy girl, but she shan't plague you while your mamma's about."

Enna cast a look of triumph at Elsie and ran off with her prize, followed by her mother, while poor Elsie hid her face in Chloe's lap and cried bitterly.

It required all Chloe's religion to keep down her anger and indignation at this unjust and cruel treatment of her darling, and for a few moments she allowed her to sob and cry without a word, only soothing her with mute caresses, not daring to trust her voice, lest her anger should find vent in words. But at length, when her feelings had grown somewhat calmer, she said soothingly, "Nebber

mind it, my poor darlin' chile. Just go to de
city and buy de prettiest purse you can find
for Miss Rose."

But Elsie shook her head sadly. "I wanted
it to be my own work," she sobbed, "and now
there is no time."

"Oh! I'll tell you what, my pet," exclaimed
Chloe, suddenly, "dere's de purse you was
a knittin' for your papa, an' dey wouldn't send
it for you; you can get dat done for de lady
and knit another for your papa 'fore he comes
home."

Elsie raised her head with a look of relief,
but her face clouded again, as she replied,
"But it is not quite done, and I haven't the
beads to finish it with, and Miss Rose goes day
after to-morrow."

"Nebber mind dat, darlin'," said Chloe,
jumping up, "Pomp he been gwine to de city
dis bery afternoon, an' we'll tell him to buy
de beads, an' den you can get de purse finished
'fore to-morrow night, an' de lady don't go till
de next day, an' so it gwine all come right yet."

"Oh! yes, that will do; dear old mammy, I'm
so glad you thought of it," said Elsie joyfully.
And rising, she went to her bureau, and un-

locking a drawer, took from it a bead purse of blue and gold, quite as handsome as the one of which she had been so ruthlessly despoiled, and rolling it up in a piece of paper, she handed it to Chloe, saying: "There, mammy, please give it to Pomp and tell him to match the beads and the silk exactly."

Chloe hastened in search of Pomp, but when she found him, he insisted that he should not have time to attend to Miss Elsie's commission and do his other errands, and Chloe, knowing that he, in common with all the other servants, was very fond of the little girl, felt satisfied that it was not merely an excuse, and therefore did not urge her request. She stood a moment in great perplexity, then suddenly exclaimed, "I'll go myself! Miss Elsie will spare me, an' I'll go right 'long wid you."

Chloe was entirely Elsie's servant, having no other business than to wait upon her and take care of her clothing and her room; and the little girl readily gave her permission to accompany Pomp and do the errand.

But it was quite late before Chloe returned, and the little girl spent the evening alone in her own room. Then in answer to her eager inquiries Chloe displayed her purchases with great satisfaction, saying, "Yes, darlin', I'se got de bery t'ings you wanted."

"Oh! yes," said Elsie, examining them with delight, "they are just right; and now I can finish it in a couple of hours."

"Time to get ready for bed now, ain't it, pet?" asked Chloe; but before the little girl had time to answer, a servant knocked at the door and handed in a note for her. It was from Miss Allison, and, hastily tearing it open, she read:

"DEAR ELSIE—I am very sorry that we cannot have our reading together this evening; but be sure, darling, to come to me early in the morning; it will be our last opportunity, for, dear child, I have another disappointment for you. I had not expected to leave before day after to-morrow, but I have learned this evening that the vessel sails a day sooner than I had supposed, and therefore I shall be obliged to start on my journey to-morrow.

"Your friend, ROSE."

Elsie dropped the note on the floor and burst into tears.

"What de matter, darlin'?" asked Chloe anxiously.

"Oh! Miss Rose, dear, *dear* Miss Rose is going to-morrow," she sobbed. Then hastily drying her eyes, she said: "But I have no time for crying. I must sit up and finish the purse to-night, because there will not be time to-morrow."

It was long past her usual hour for retiring when at last her task, or rather her labor of love, was completed. Yet she was up betimes, and at the usual hour her gentle rap was heard at Miss Allison's door.

Rose clasped her in her arms and kissed her.

"O Miss Rose! *dear, dear* Miss Rose, what shall I do without you?" sobbed the little girl. "I shall have nobody to love me now but mammy."

"You have another and a better Friend, dear Elsie, Who has said, 'I will never leave thee, nor forsake thee,'" whispered Rose, with another tender caress.

"Yes," said Elsie, wiping away her tears; "and He is your Friend, too; and don't you think, Miss Rose, He will bring us together again some day?"

"My poor darling!" Rose said, "we will hope to meet again before very long. Who knows but your papa may come home, and some day bring you to see me. It seems not unlikely, as he is so fond of traveling."

Elsie looked up, smiling through her tears. "Oh! how delightful that would be," she said. "But it seems as though my papa would never come," she added, with a deep-drawn sigh.

"Well, darling, we can hope," Rose answered cheerfully. "And I shall write to you. I will write on my journey, if I can, so that you will get the letter in a week from the time I leave; and then you must write to me; will you?"

"If you won't care for the mistakes, Miss Rose. But you know I am a very little girl, and I wouldn't like to let Miss Day read my letter to you, to correct it. But I shall be so very glad to get yours. I never had a letter in my life."

"I shan't care for mistakes at all, dear, and no one shall see your letters but myself," said Rose, kissing her. "I should be as sorry as you to have Miss Day look at them."

Elsie drew out the purse and put it in her friend's hand, saying: "It is all my own work, dear Miss Rose; I thought you would value it more for that."

"And indeed I shall, darling," replied Rose, with tears of pleasure in her eyes. "It is beautiful in itself, but I shall value it ten times more because it is your gift and the work of your own dear little hands."

But the breakfast bell now summoned them to join the rest of the family, and, in a few moments after they left the table, the carriage which was to take Rose to the city was at the door. Rose had endeared herself to all, old and young, and they were loath to part with her. One after another bade her an affectionate farewell. Elsie was the last. Rose pressed her tenderly to her bosom and kissed her again and again, saying, in a voice half choked with grief, "God bless and keep you, my poor little darling; my dear, dear little Elsie!"

Elsie could not speak; and the moment the carriage had rolled away with her friend, she went to her own room, and locking herself in, cried long and bitterly. She had learned to love Rose very dearly, and to lean upon her very much; and now the parting from her, with no certainty of ever meeting her again in this world, was the severest trial the poor child had ever known.

Chapter 3

The morning blush was lighted up by hope—
The hope of meeting him.
                                        —MISS LANDON

Unkindness, do thy office; poor heart, break.

A WEEK had now passed away since Miss Allison's departure, and Elsie, to whom it had been a sad and lonely one, was beginning to look eagerly for her first letter.

"It is just a week to-day since Rose left," remarked Adelaide at the breakfast table, "and I think we ought to hear from her soon. She promised to write on her journey. Ah! here comes Pomp with the letters now," she added, as the servant man entered the room bearing in his hand the bag in which he always brought the letters of the family from the office in the neighboring city.

"Do make haste, papa, and see if there is not one from Rose," said Adelaide coaxingly, as her father took the bag and very deliberately adjusted his spectacles before opening it.

"Have patience, young lady," said he. "Yes,

49

here is a letter for you, and one for Elsie,"
tossing them across the table as he spoke.

Elsie eagerly seized hers and ran away to
her own room to read it.

She had just finished its perusal and was
beginning it again, when she heard Adelaide's
voice calling her by name, and the next moment she entered the room, saying: "Well,
Elsie, I suppose you have read your letter;
and now I have another piece of news for you.
Can you guess what it is?" she asked, looking
at her with a strange smile.

"Oh, no, Aunt Adelaide; please tell me. Is
dear Miss Rose coming back?"

"Oh! nonsense; what a guess!" said Adelaide.
"No, stranger than that. My brother Horace
—your father—has actually sailed for Amer-
ica and is coming directly home."

Elsie sprang up, her cheeks flushed and her
little heart beating wildly.

"O Aunt Adelaide!" she cried, "is it really
true? is he coming? and will he be here soon?"

"He has really started at last; but how soon
he will be here I don't know," replied her aunt,
turning to leave the room. "I have told you
all I know about it."

Elsie clasped her hands together and sank down upon a sofa, Miss Rose's letter, prized so highly a moment before, lying unheeded at her feet; for her thoughts were far away, following that unknown parent as he crossed the ocean; trying to imagine how he would look, how he would speak, what would be his feelings toward her.

"Oh!" she asked, with a beating heart, "*will* he *love* me? My own papa! will he let me love him? will he take me in his arms and call me his own darling child?"

Elsie's lessons were but indifferently recited that morning, and Miss Day frowned, and said in a tone of severity that it did not agree with her to receive letters; and that, unless she wished her papa to be much displeased with her on his expected arrival, she must do a great deal better than that.

She had touched the right chord then; for Elsie, intensely anxious to please that unknown father, and, if possible, gain his approbation and affection, gave her whole mind to her studies with such a determined purpose that the governess could find no more cause for complaint.

Horace Dinsmore was, like his father, an upright, moral man, who paid an outward respect to the forms of religion, but cared nothing for the vital power of godliness; trusted entirely to his morality, and looked upon Christians as hypocrites and deceivers. He had been told that his little Elsie was one of them, and, though he would not have acknowledged it even to himself, it had prejudiced him against her.

Horace himself had come to look upon his early marriage as a piece of boyish folly, of which he was rather ashamed; and so constantly had Mr. Dinsmore spoken in his letters of Elsie as "old Grayson's grandchild," that he had got into the habit of looking upon her as a kind of disgrace to him; especially as she had always been described to him as a disagreeable, troublesome child.

He had loved his wife with all the warmth of his passionate nature and had mourned bitterly over her untimely death; but years of study, travel, and worldly pleasures had almost banished her image from his mind, and he seldom thought of her except in connection with the child for whom he felt a secret dislike.

Scarcely anything but the expected arrival was now spoken or thought of at Roselands, and at length a letter came telling them that they might look upon it as being but one day in advance of its writer.

"O mammy, mammy!" exclaimed Elsie, jumping up and down and clapping her hands for joy, "just think! papa, dear papa, will be here to-morrow morning."

She seemed wild with delight; but suddenly sobered down, and a look of care stole over the little face, as the torturing question recurred to her mind, *Will he love me?*

Just at that moment an unusual bustle was heard in the house.

Elsie started, changed color, and stood listening with a throbbing heart.

Presently little feet were heard running rapidly down the hall, and Walter, throwing open the door, called out, "Elsie, he's come!" and catching her hand, hurried her along to the parlor door.

"Stop, stop, Walter," she gasped, as they reached it; and she leaned against the wall, her heart throbbing so wildly she could scarcely breathe.

"What is the matter?" said he. "Are you ill? Come along!" and pushing the door open, he rushed in, dragging her after him.

Everything in the room seemed to be turning round, and for an instant she scarcely knew where she was.

But a strange voice asked, "And who is this?" and looking up as her grandfather pronounced her name, she saw a stranger standing before her—very youthful-looking and very handsome—who exclaimed hastily, "What! this great girl *my* child? Really it is enough to make a man feel old."

Then, taking her hand, he stooped and coldly kissed her lips.

She was trembling violently, and the very depth of her feelings kept her silent and still; her hand lay still in his, cold and clammy.

He held it an instant, at the same time gazing searchingly into her face; then dropped it, saying in a tone of displeasure, "I am not an ogre, that you need be so afraid of me; but there, you may go; I will not keep you in terror any longer."

She rushed away to her own room, and there, throwing herself upon the bed, wept long and wildly. It was the disappointment of a lifelong hope. Since her earliest recollection she had looked and longed for this hour; and it seemed as though the little heart would break with its weight of bitter anguish.

She was all alone, for Chloe had gone down to the kitchen to talk over the arrival, not doubting that her darling was supremely happy in the possession of her long-looked-for parent.

And so the little girl lay there with her crushed and bleeding heart, sobbing, mourning, weeping as though she would weep her very life away without an earthly friend to speak one word of comfort.

"O papa, papa!" she sobbed, "my own papa, you do not love me; me, your own little girl. Oh! my heart will break. O mamma, mamma! if I could only go to you; for there is no one here to love me, and I am so lonely, oh, *so* lonely and desolate."

And thus Chloe found her, when she came in an hour later, weeping and sobbing out such broken exclamations of grief and anguish.

She was much surprised, but comprehending at once how her child was suffering, she raised her up in her strong arms, and laying the little head lovingly against her bosom, she smoothed the tangled hair, kissed the tear-swollen eyes, and bathed the throbbing temples, saying, "My precious pet, my darlin' chile, your ole mammy loves you better dan life; an' did my darlin' forget de almighty Friend dat says, '*I* have loved thee with an everlasting love,' an' 'I will never leave thee, nor forsake thee'? He sticks closer dan a brudder, precious chile, and says, 'though a woman forget her sucking child, He will not forget *His* chillen.' Mothers love dere chillens better dan fathers, darlin', and so you see Jesus' love is better dan all other love; an' I *knows* you hes got dat."

"O mammy! ask Him to take me to Himself and to mamma—for oh! I am very lonely and I want to die!"

"Hush, hush, darlin'; old Chloe nebber could ask dat; dis ole heart would break for sure; and you know we must wait de Lord's time."

"O mammy!" she said, "ask Him to make my father love me."

"I will, darlin', I will," sobbed Chloe,

pressing the little form closer to her heart, "an' don't you go for to be discouraged right away; for I'se sure Massa Horace must love you 'fore long."

The tea bell rang, and the family gathered about the table; but one chair remained unoccupied.

"Where is Miss Elsie?" asked Adelaide of one of the servants.

"Dunno, missus," was the reply.

"Well, then, go and see," said Adelaide, "perhaps she did not hear the bell."

The servant returned in a moment, saying that Miss Elsie had a bad headache and did not want any supper. Mr. Horace Dinsmore paused in the conversation he was carrying on with his father, to listen to the servant's announcement. "I hope she is not a sickly child," said he, addressing Adelaide, "is she subject to such attacks?"

"Not very," replied his sister, dryly, for she had seen the meeting and felt really sorry for Elsie's evident disappointment, "I imagine crying has brought this on."

He colored violently and said in a tone of great displeasure, "Truly, the return of a parent *is* a cause for grief; yet I hardly expected my presence to be quite so distressing to my only child. I had no idea that she had already learned to dislike me so thoroughly."

"She doesn't," said Adelaide. "She has been looking and longing for your return ever since I have known her."

"Then she has certainly been disappointed in me; her grief is not at all complimentary, explain it as you will."

Adelaide made no reply, for she saw that he was determined to put an unfavorable construction upon Elsie's conduct, and feared tha any defense she could offer would only increase his displeasure.

It was with a trembling heart, hoping yet fearing, longing and yet dreading to see her father, that Elsie descended to the breakfast room the next morning. She glanced timidly around, but he was not there.

"Where is papa, Aunt Adelaide?" she asked.

"He is not coming down to breakfast, as he feels quite fatigued with his journey," replied her aunt, "so you will not see him this morning, and perhaps not at all to-day, for there will be a good deal of company here this afternoon and evening."

Elsie sighed and looked sadly disappointed. She found it very difficult to attend to her lessons that morning, and every time the door opened she started and looked up, half hoping it might be her papa.

But he did not come; and so she saw nothing of her father that day.

But the next morning Chloe told her the children were to breakfast with the family, as all the visitors had left excepting one or two gentlemen. So Elsie went down to the breakfast room, where, to her surprise, she found her papa sitting alone, reading the morning paper.

He looked up as she entered.

"Good morning, papa," she said, in half-trembling tones. He started a little—for it was the first time he had ever been addressed by that title—gave her a glance of mingled curiosity and interest, half held out his hand, but drawing it back again, simply said, "Good morning, Elsie," and returned to his paper.

But just at that instant the door opened, and Enna, looking rosy and happy, came running in, and rushing up to her brother, climbed upon his knee and put her arms around his neck, saying, "Good morning, Brother Horace. I want a kiss."

"You shall have it, little pet," said he, throwing down his paper.

Then, kissing her several times and hugging her in his arms, he said, *"You* are not afraid of me, are you? nor sorry that I have come home?"

"No, indeed," said Enna.

He glanced at Elsie as she stood looking at them, her large, soft eyes full of tears. She could not help feeling that Enna had her place and was receiving the caresses that should have been lavished upon herself.

"Jealous," thought her father, "I cannot bear jealous people"; and he gave her a look of displeasure that cut her to the heart, and she turned quickly away and left the room to hide the tears she could no longer keep back.

"I am envious," she thought, "jealous of Enna. Oh! how wicked!" And she prayed silently, "Dear Saviour, help me! take away these sinful feelings."

Young as she was, she was learning to have

*Enna climbed upon his knee, saying,
"Good morning. I want a kiss."*

some control over her feelings, and in a few moments she had so far recovered her composure as to be able to return to the breakfast room and take her place at the table.

Her father took no further notice of her, and she did not dare trust herself to look at him. She scarcely raised her eyes from her plate, and did not know how often a strange gentleman who sat nearly opposite fixed his upon her.

As she left the room at the conclusion of the meal, he asked, while following her with his eyes, "Is that one of your sisters, Dinsmore?"

"No," said he, coloring slightly, "she is my daughter."

"Ah, indeed!" said his friend. "I remember to have heard that you had a child, but had forgotten it. Well, you have no reason to be ashamed of her; she is lovely, perfectly lovely! has the sweetest little face I ever saw."

"Will you ride, Travilla?" asked Mr. Dinsmore hastily, as though anxious to change the subject.

"I don't care if I do," was the reply, and they went out together.

Some hours later in the day Elsie was at the piano in the music room practicing, when a sudden feeling that someone was in the room caused her to turn and look behind her.

Mr. Travilla was standing there.

"Excuse me," said he, bowing politely, "but I heard the sound of the instrument and ventured to walk in."

Elsie was very modest and rather timid, too, but also very polite; so she said, "No excuse is necessary; but will you not take a seat, sir? though I fear my music will not afford you any pleasure, for you know I am only a little girl and cannot play very well yet."

"Thank you," said he, taking a seat by her side. "And now will you do me the favor to repeat the song I heard you singing a few moments since?"

Elsie immediately complied. She had a very fine voice for a child of her age; its sweetness was remarkable, both in singing and speaking; and she had also a good deal of musical talent, which had been well cultivated, for she had had good teachers, and had practiced with great patience and perseverance. Her music was simple, as suited her years, but her performance of it was very good indeed.

Mr. Travilla thanked her very heartily and complimented her singing; then asked for another and another song, another and another piece, chatting with her about each until they grew quite familiar, and Elsie lost all feeling of embarrassment.

"Elsie, I think, is your name, is it not?" he asked, after a little.

"Yes, sir," said she, "Elsie Dinsmore."

"And you are the daughter of my friend, Mr. Horace Dinsmore?"

"Yes, sir."

"Your papa has been absent a long time, and I suppose you must have quite forgotten him."

"No, sir, not *forgotten,* for I never had seen him."

"Indeed!" said he in a tone of surprise, "then, since he is an entire stranger to you, I suppose you cannot have much love for him?"

Elsie raised her large, dark eyes to his face with an expression of astonishment. "Not love papa, my own dear papa, who has no child but me? Oh! sir, how could you think that?"

"Ah! I see I was mistaken," said he, smiling, "I thought you could hardly care for him at all; but do you think that he loves you?"

Elsie dropped her face into her hands and burst into an agony of tears.

The young gentleman looked extremely vexed with himself.

"My poor little girl, my poor, dear little girl," he said, stroking her hair, "forgive me. I am very, *very* sorry for my thoughtless question. Do be comforted, my poor child, for whether your papa loves you now or not, I am quite sure he soon will."

Elsie now dried her tears, rose and closed the instrument. He assisted her, and then asked if she would not take a little walk with him in the garden. She complied, and, feeling really very sorry for the wound he had so thoughtlessly inflicted, as well as interested in his little companion, he exerted all his powers to entertain her—talked with her about the plants and flowers, described those he had seen in foreign lands, and related incidents of travel, usually choosing those in which her father had borne a part, because he perceived that they were doubly interesting to her.

When the dinner bell rang he led her in and seated her by himself, and never was any lady more carefully waited upon than little Elsie at this meal. Once she looked timidly at her father, and her eyes met his. He was looking at her with an expression half curious, half amused. She was at a loss to understand the look, but, satisfied that there was no displeasure in it, her heart grew light, and her cheeks flushed with happiness.

"Really, Dinsmore," said Mr. Travilla, as they stood together near one of the windows of the drawing room soon after dinner, "your little girl is remarkably intelligent, as well as remarkably pretty; and I have discovered that she has quite a good deal of musical talent."

"Indeed! I think it is quite a pity that she does not belong to you, Travilla, instead of me, since you seem to appreciate her so much more highly," replied the father, laughing.

"I wish she did," said his friend. "But, seriously, Dinsmore, you ought to love that child, for she certainly loves you devotedly."

He looked surprised. "How do you know?" he asked.

"It was evident enough from what I saw

and heard this morning. Dinsmore, she would value a caress from you more than the richest jewel."

"Doubtful," replied Horace, hastily quitting the room, for Elsie had come out onto the portico in her riding suit, and Jim, her usual attendant, was bringing up her horse.

"Are you going to ride, Elsie?" asked her father, coming up to her.

"Yes, papa," she said, raising her eyes to his face.

He lifted her in his arms and placed her on the horse, saying to the servant as he did so, "Now, Jim, you must take good care of my little girl."

Tears of happiness rose in Elsie's eyes as she turned her horse's head and rode down the avenue. "He called me *his* little girl," she murmured to herself, "and bade Jim take good care of me. Oh! he *will* love me soon, as good, kind Mr. Travilla said he would."

Her father was still standing on the portico, looking after her.

"How well she sits her horse!" remarked Travilla, who had stepped out and stood close by his side.

"Yes, I think she does," was the reply, in an absent tone. He was thinking of a time, some eight or nine years before, when he had assisted another Elsie to mount her horse and had ridden for hours at her side.

All the afternoon memories of the past came crowding thickly on his mind, and an emotion of tenderness began to spring up in his heart toward the child of her who had once been so dear to him; and as he saw the little girl ride up to the house on her return, he again went out, and lifting her from her horse, asked kindly, "Had you a pleasant ride, my dear?"

"Oh! yes, papa, very pleasant," she said, looking up at him with a face beaming with delight.

He stooped and kissed her, saying, "I think I shall ride with you one of these days; should you like it?"

"Oh! so very, *very* much, papa," she answered eagerly.

He smiled at her earnestness, and she hastened away to her room to change her dress and tell Chloe of her happiness.

More company came, so that the drawing

room was quite full in the evening; and, though Elsie was there, her father seemed too much occupied with the guests to give her even a glance. She sat alone and unnoticed in a corner, her eyes following him wherever he moved, and her ear strained to catch every tone of his voice, until Mr. Travilla came up to her and led her to a pleasant-looking elderly lady, who sat at a table examining some choice engravings which Mr. Dinsmore had brought with him from Europe.

"Mother," said Mr. Travilla, "this is my little friend Elsie."

"Ah!" said she, giving the little girl a kiss, "I am glad to see you, my dear."

Mr. Travilla set a chair for her close to his mother and then sat down on her other side, and taking up the engravings one after another, he explained them to her in a most entertaining manner, generally having some anecdote to tell in connection with each.

Elsie was so much amused and delighted with what he was saying that she at last quite forgot her father, and did not notice where he was.

Suddenly Mr. Travilla laid down the engraving he had in his hand, saying: "Come, Miss Elsie, I want my mother to hear you play and sing; will you not do me the favor to repeat that song I admired so much this morning?"

"Oh! Mr. Travilla!" exclaimed the little girl, blushing and trembling, "I could not play or sing before so many people. Please excuse me."

"Elsie," said her father's voice, just at her side, *go immediately*, and do as the gentleman requests."

His tone was very stern, and as she lifted her eyes to his face, she saw that his look was still more so; and tremblingly and tearfully she rose to obey.

"Stay," said Mr. Travilla kindly, pitying her distress, "I withdraw my request."

"But I do *not* withdraw my command," said her father in the same stern tone. "Go at once, Elsie, and do as I bid you."

She obeyed instantly.

Mr. Travilla, scolding himself inwardly all the time for having brought her into such trouble, selected her music, and placing it before her as she took her seat at the instrument, whispered encouragingly, "Now, Miss Elsie, only have confidence in yourself; that is all that is necessary to your success."

Elsie was not only embarrassed, but her heart was well-nigh broken by her father's sternness, and the tears *would* fill her eyes so that she could see neither notes nor words. She attempted to play the prelude, but blundered sadly, her embarrassment increasing every moment.

"Never mind the prelude, but just begin the song," said Mr. Travilla.

She made the attempt, but fairly broke down, and burst into tears before she had got through the first verse. Her father had come up behind her and was standing there, looking much mortified.

"Elsie," he said, leaning down and speaking in a low, stern tone, close to her ear, "I am ashamed of you; go to your room and to your bed immediately."

With a heart almost bursting with grief and mortification she obeyed him, and her pillow was wet with many bitter tears before the weary eyes closed in slumber.

When she came down the next morning, she

learned that Mr. Travilla and his mother had returned to their own home; she was very sorry she had not been permitted to say good-bye to her friend, and for several days she felt very sad and lonely, for all her father's coldness of manner had returned, and he scarcely ever spoke to her.

How to gain her father's love was the constant subject of her thoughts, and she tried in many ways to win his affection. She always yielded a ready and cheerful obedience to his commands, and strove to anticipate and fulfill all his wishes. But he seldom noticed her, unless to give a command or administer a rebuke, while he lavished many a caress upon his little sister Enna. Often Elsie would watch him fondling her, until unable any longer to control her feelings, she would rush away to her own room to weep and mourn in secret, and pray that her father might some day learn to love her.

Chapter 4

With more capacity for love than earth
Bestows on most of mortal mould and birth.
—BYRON

What are our hopes?
Like garlands, on affliction's forehead worn,
Kissed in the morning, and at evening torn.
—DAVENPORT'S *King John and Matilda*

ELSIE was seated at her desk in the school-room one morning when a servant entered and handed a card to the governess.

Miss Day glanced at it and said: "Elsie, your father wants you. You may go."

Elsie rose in some trepidation and left the room, wondering what her papa could want with her.

"Where is papa, Fanny?" she asked.

"In de drawin' room, Miss Elsie," was the reply; and she hastened to seek him there.

He held out his hand as she entered, saying with a smile, "Come here, daughter."

It was the first time he had called her that, and it sent a thrill of joy to her heart.

"I am going to drive over to Ion, where your friend Mr. Travilla lives, to spend the day; would my little daughter like to go with me?"

"Oh! so *very* much, papa!" she answered eagerly.

"There are no little folks there," he said, smiling, "nobody to see but Mr. Travilla and his mother. But I see you want to go; so run and ask Aunt Chloe to get you ready. Tell her I want you nicely dressed, and the carriage will be at the door in half an hour."

Elsie bounded away to do his bidding, her face radiant with happiness; and at the specified time came down again, looking so very lovely that her father gazed at her with proud delight, and could not refrain from giving her a kiss as he lifted her up to place her in the carriage.

Then, seating himself beside her, he took her hand in his; and, closing the door with the other, bade the coachman drive on.

"I suppose you have never been to Ion, Elsie?" he said inquiringly.

"No, sir; but I have heard Aunt Adelaide say she thought it a very pretty place," replied the little girl.

"So it is—almost as pretty as Roselands,"

said her father. "Travilla and I have known each other from boyhood, and I spent many a happy day at Ion, and we had many a boyish frolic together before I ever thought of you."

Elsie's eyes sparkled. "O papa!" she said eagerly, "won't you tell me about those times? It seems so strange that you ever were a little boy and I was nowhere."

He laughed, then said musingly, "It seems but a very little while to me, Elsie, since I was no older than you are now."

He sighed and relapsed into silence.

They rode on quietly for some time, until a squirrel darting up a tree caught Elsie's eye, and she uttered an exclamation. "O papa! did you see that squirrel? Look at him now, perched up on that branch."

This reminded Mr. Dinsmore of a day he had spent in those woods hunting squirrels, when a boy, and he gave Elsie an animated account of it. One of the incidents of the day had been the accidental discharge of the fowling piece of one of his young companions close at Horace Dinsmore's side, missing him by but a hair's breadth.

"I felt faint and sick when I knew how near

I had been to death," he said, as he finished his narrative.

Elsie had been listening with breathless interest.

"Dear papa," she murmured, laying her little cheek against his hand, "how good God was to spare your life! If you had been killed I could never have had you for my papa."

"Perhaps you might have had a much better one, Elsie," he said gravely.

"Oh! no, papa, I wouldn't want any other," she replied earnestly, pressing his hand to her lips.

"Ah! here we are," exclaimed her father, as at that instant the carriage turned into a broad avenue, up which they drove quite rapidly, and the next moment they had stopped, the coachman had thrown open the carriage door, and Mr. Dinsmore, springing out, lifted his little girl in his arms and set her down on the steps of the veranda.

"Ah! Dinsmore, how do you do? Glad to see you and my little friend Elsie, too," cried Mr. Travilla, as, hurrying out to welcome them, he shook Mr. Dinsmore cordially by the hand and kissed Elsie's cheek.

walk in," he continued, leading
the house, "my mother will be
see you both."

ravilla's greeting was less boister-
inly was not lacking in cordiality,
and she made Elsie feel at home at once.

The gentlemen soon went out together, and
Elsie spent the morning in Mrs. Travilla's
room, chatting with her and assisting her with
some coarse garments she was making for her
servants.

Mrs. Travilla was an earnest Christian, and
the lady and the little girl were not long in
discovering the tie which existed between
them.

Mrs. Travilla, being also a woman of great
discernment, and having known Horace Dinsmore nearly all his life, had conceived a very
correct idea of the trials and difficulties of
Elsie's situation, and without alluding to them
at all, gave her some most excellent advice.

They were still chatting together when Mr.
Travilla came in, saying, "Come, Elsie, I want
to take you out to see my garden and hothouse.
We will just have time before dinner. Will
you go along, mother?"

"No; I have some little matters to attend to before dinner, and will leave you to do the honors," replied the lady; and taking the little girl's hand, he led her out.

"Where is papa?" asked Elsie.

"Oh! he's in the library, looking over some new books," replied Mr. Travilla. "He always cared more for books than anything else. But what do you think of my flowers?"

"Oh! they are lovely! What a variety you have! what a splendid Cape jessamine that is, and there is a variety of cactus I never saw before! Oh! you have a great many more, and handsomer, I think, than we have at Rose-lands," exclaimed Elsie, as she passed admiringly from one to another.

Mr. Travilla was much pleased with the admiration she expressed, for he was very fond of his flowers.

But they were soon called in to dinner, where Elsie was seated by her father.

"I hope this little girl has not given you any trouble, Mrs. Travilla," said he, looking gravely at her.

"Oh! no," the lady hastened to say, "I have enjoyed her coming very much indeed, and hope you will bring her to see me again soon."

After dinner, as the day was very warm, they adjourned to the veranda, which was the coolest place to be found. But the conversation was upon some subject which did not interest Elsie, and she presently stole away to the library and seating herself in a corner of the sofa, was soon lost to everything around her in the intense interest with which she was reading a book she had taken from the table.

"Ah! that is what you are about, Miss Elsie! a bookworm, just like your father, I see. I had been wondering what had become of you for the last two hours," exclaimed Mr. Travilla's pleasant voice; and, sitting down beside her, he took the book from her hand, and putting it behind him, said, "Put it away now; you will have time enough to finish it, and I want you to talk to me."

"Oh! please let me have it," she pleaded. "I shall not have much time, for papa will soon be calling me to go home."

"No, no, he is not to take you away; I have made a bargain with him to let me keep you," said Mr. Travilla very gravely. "We both think that there are children enough at Roselands without you; and so your papa has given you to me; and you are to be *my* little girl, and call *me* papa in future."

Elsie gazed earnestly in his face for an instant, saying in a half-frightened tone, "You are only joking, Mr. Travilla."

"Not a bit of it," said he. "Can't you see that I'm in earnest?"

His tone and look were both so serious that for an instant Elsie believed he meant all that he was saying, and springing to her feet with a little cry of alarm, she hastily withdrew her hand which he had taken, and rushing out to the veranda, where her father still sat conversing with Mrs. Travilla, she flung herself into his arms, and clinging to him, hid her face on his breast, sobbing, "O papa, *dear* papa! *don't* give me away; *please* don't—I will be so good—I will do everything you bid me—I——"

"Why, Elsie, what does all this mean?" exclaimed Mr. Dinsmore in great surprise and perplexity, while Mr. Travilla stood in the doorway looking half amused, half sorry for what he had done.

"O papa!" sobbed the little girl, still clinging to him as though fearing she should be torn from his arms, "Mr. Travilla says you have given me to him. O papa! *don't* give me away."

"Pooh! nonsense, Elsie! I am ashamed of you! How can you be so very silly as to believe for one moment anything so perfectly absurd as that I should think of giving you away? Why, I would as soon think of parting with my eyes."

Elsie raised her head and gazed searchingly into his face; then, with a deep-drawn sigh of relief, dropped it again, saying, "Oh! I am *so* glad."

"Really, Miss Elsie," said Travilla, coming up and patting her on the shoulder, "I can't say that I feel much complimented; and, indeed, I don't see why you need have been so very much distressed at the prospect before you; for I must say I have vanity enough to imagine that I should make the better—or, at least, the more indulgent—father of the two. Come, now, wouldn't you be willing to try me for a month, if your papa will give consent?"

Elsie shook her head.

"I will let you have your own way in everything," urged Travilla coaxingly, "and I know that is more than he does."

"I don't want my own way, Mr. Travilla; I know it wouldn't always be a good way," replied Elsie decidedly.

Her father laughed and passed his hand caressingly over her curls.

"I thought you liked me, little Elsie," said Travilla in a tone of disappointment.

"So I do, Mr. Travilla; I like you very much," she replied.

"Well, don't you think I would make a good father?"

"I am sure you would be very kind, and that I should love you very much; but not so much as I love my own papa; because, you know, you are *not* my papa and never can be, even if he *should* give me to you."

Mr. Dinsmore laughed heartily, saying, "I think you may as well give it up, Travilla; it seems I'll have to keep her whether or no, for she clings to me like a leech."

"Well, Elsie, you will at least come to the piano and play a little for me, will you not?" asked Travilla, smiling.

But Elsie still clung to her father, seeming

loath to leave him until he said in his grave, decided way, "Go, Elsie; go at once and do as you are requested."

Then she rose instantly to obey.

Travilla looked somewhat vexed. "I wish," he afterward remarked to his mother, "that Dinsmore was not quite so ready to second my requests with his commands. I want Elsie's compliance to be voluntary; else I think it worth very little."

Elsie played and sang until they were called to tea, after which she sat quietly by her father's side, listening to the conversation of her elders until the carriage was announced.

"Well, my daughter," said Mr. Dinsmore, when they were fairly upon their way to Roselands, "have you had a pleasant day?"

"Oh, *very* pleasant, papa, excepting——"
She paused, looking a little embarrassed.

"Well, excepting what?" he asked, smiling.

"Excepting when Mr. Travilla frightened me so, papa," she replied, moving closer to him.

"And you do love your own papa best and don't want to exchange him for another?" he said inquiringly, as he passed his arm affectionately around her waist.

"Oh! no, dear papa, not for anybody else in all the world," she said earnestly.

He made no reply in words, but, looking highly gratified, bent down and kissed her cheek.

He did not speak again during their ride, but when the carriage stopped he lifted her out, and setting her gently down, bade her a kind good-night, saying it was time for mammy to put her to bed.

She ran lightly upstairs, and springing into her nurse's arms, exclaimed: "O mammy, mammy! I am happy, oh! *so* happy, because I do believe that papa is beginning to love me a little, and I hope that perhaps after a while he will love me very much."

Chapter 5

Man is unjust, but God is just; and finally justice
triomphs.
—LONGFELLOW'S *Evangeline*

How disappointment tracks
The steps of hope!
—MISS LANDON

ONE afternoon the younger members of the
family, Arthur, Elsie, Walter, and Enna, were
setting out to take a walk, when Elsie, seeing
a gold chain depending from the pocket of
Arthur's jacket, exclaimed: "O Arthur! how
could you take grandpa's watch? *Do* put it
away, for you will be almost sure to injure it."

"Hold your tongue, Elsie; I'll do as I
please," was the polite rejoinder.

"But, Arthur, you *know* that grandpa would
never let you take it. I have often heard him
say that it was very valuable, for it was seldom
that so good a one could be had at any price;
and I know that he paid a great deal for the
watch."

"Well, if he prizes it so, he needn't have
left it lying on his table, and so I'll just teach

him a lesson. It's about time he learned to be careful."

"O Arthur! do put it away," pleaded Elsie, "if anything should happen to it, what will grandpa say?"

Arthur would not listen to her remonstrances.

The walk was far from being a pleasure that afternoon; the boys ran so fast that it quite put Elsie out of breath to keep up with them; and then every little while Arthur would cut some caper that made her tremble for the watch.

At length, while he was in the act of climbing a tree, the watch dropped from his pocket and fell to the ground, striking with considerable force.

Elsie uttered a scream, and Arthur, now thoroughly frightened himself, jumped down and picked it up.

The crystal was broken, the back dented, and how much the works were injured they could not tell; but it had ceased to run.

"O Arthur! see what you've done!" exclaimed Walter.

"What will papa say?" said Enna, while

"If any of you dare tell of me, I'll make
you sorry for it," exclaimed Arthur.

Elsie stood pale and trembling, not speaking a word.

"You hush!" exclaimed Arthur fiercely. "I'll tell you what, if any of you dare tell of me, I'll make you sorry for it to the last day of your life. Do you hear?"

The question was addressed to Elsie in a tone of defiance.

"Arthur," said she, "grandpa will know that *somebody* did it, and surely you would not wish an innocent person to be punished for *your* fault."

"I don't care *who* gets punished, so that papa does not find out that I did it," said he, "and if you dare to tell of me, I'll pay you for it."

When they reached the house, Arthur replaced the watch on his father's table, whence he had taken it, and then they all awaited his return with what courage they might.

"I say, Wally," said Arthur, drawing his little brother aside and speaking in a low tone, having first sent a cautious glance around to assure himself that no one else was within hearing, "I say, what would you give me for that new riding whip of mine?"

"O Arthur! anything I've got," exclaimed the little boy, eagerly. "But you wouldn't give it up, I know, and you're only trying to tease me."

"No, indeed, Wal; I mean to *give* it to you if you'll only be a good fellow and do as I tell you."

"What?" he asked with intense interest.

"Tell papa that Jim broke the watch."

"But he *didn't*," replied the child, opening his eyes wide with astonishment.

"Well, what of that, you little goose?" exclaimed Arthur impatiently. "Papa doesn't know that."

"But Jim will get punished," said Walter, "and I don't want to tell such a big story either."

"Very well, sir, then you'll not get the whip; and, besides, if you don't do as I wish, I'm certain you'll see a ghost one of these nights; for there's one comes to see me sometimes, and I'll send him right off to you."

"Oh! *don't*, Arthur, don't; I'd die of fright," cried the little boy, who was very timid, glancing nervously around, as if he expected the ghost to appear immediately.

"I tell you I will, though, if you don't do as I say; he'll come this very night and carry you off, and never bring you back."

"O Arthur! don't let him come, and I'll say anything you want me to," cried the little fellow in great terror.

"That's a good boy; I knew you would," said Arthur, smiling triumphantly. And turning away from Walter, he next sought out Enna, and tried his threats and persuasions upon her with even better success.

It was still early in the evening when Mr. and Mrs. Dinsmore returned—for once bringing no company with them; and he had not been many minutes in the house before he took up his watch, and of course instantly discovered the injury it had sustained.

His suspicions at once fell upon Arthur, whose character for mischief was well established; and burning with rage, watch in hand, he went to the drawing room, which he entered, asking in tones tremulous with passion, "Where is Arthur? Young rascal! this is some of *his* work," he added, holding up the broken watch.

"My dear, how can you say so? have you

any proof?" asked his wife deprecatingly, adding in her softest tones, "My poor boy seems to get the blame of everything that goes wrong."

"He gets no more than he deserves," replied her husband angrily. "Arthur! Arthur, I say, where are you?"

"He is in the garden, sir, I think," said Mr. Horace Dinsmore.

The father instantly despatched a servant to bring him in, sending a second in search of the overseer, while a third was ordered to assemble all the house servants. "I will sift this matter to the bottom, and child or servant, the guilty one shall certainly suffer for it," exclaimed the old gentleman, angrily pacing the room. "Arthur," said he, sternly, as the boy made his appearance, looking somewhat pale and alarmed, "how dare you meddle with my watch?"

"I didn't, sir; I never touched it," he replied boldly, yet avoiding his father's eye as he uttered the deliberate falsehood.

"There, my dear, I told you so," exclaimed his mother triumphantly.

"I don't believe you," said his father, "and

if you are guilty, as I strongly suspect, you had better confess it at once, before I find it out in some other way."

"I didn't do it, sir. It was Jim, and I can prove it by Walter and Enna; we all saw it fall from his pocket when he was up in a tree, and he cried like anything when he found it was broken, and said he didn't mean to do it any harm; he was only going to wear it a little while, and then put it back all safe; but now master would be dreadfully angry and have him flogged."

"That I will, if it is true," exclaimed the old gentleman passionately, "he shall be well whipped and set out to work on the plantation."

He looked at Enna. "What do you know of this?" he asked.

"It is true, papa, I saw him do it," she replied with a slight blush, and sending an uneasy glance around the room.

"Did you see it, too, Walter?" asked his father.

"Yes, sir," replied the little fellow in a low, reluctant tone, "but please, papa, don't punish him. I'm sure he didn't mean to break it."

"Hold your tongue! He *shall* be punished as he deserves," cried the old gentleman furiously. "Here, sir," turning to the overseer and pointing to Jim, "take the fellow out and give him such a flogging as he will remember."

Elsie was sitting in her own room, trying to learn a lesson for the next day, when she was startled by the sudden entrance of Aunt Chloe, who was sobbing violently.

"O mammy, mammy! what's the matter? has anything happened to you?" inquired the little girl, starting to her feet and dropping her book in her haste and fright.

"Why," sobbed Chloe, "Jim, he's been an' gone an' broke ole master's watch, an' he's gwine be whipped, an' old Aunt Phoebe she's cryin' fit to break her ole heart 'bout her boy, kase——"

Elsie waited to hear no more, but darting out into the hall and encountering her father on his way to his room, she rushed up to him, pale and agitated, and seizing his hand, looked up eagerly into his face, exclaiming with a burst of tears and sobs, "O papa, papa! don't oh! *don't* let them whip poor Jim."

Mr. Dinsmore's countenance was grave.

"I am sorry it is necessary, daughter," he said, "but Jim has done very wrong and deserves his punishment."

"Oh! no, papa, he did not, *indeed* he did not break the watch. I *know* he didn't, for I was by and saw it all."

"Is it *possible?*" said he in a tone of surprise, "then tell me who did do it. It could not have been you, Elsie?" and he looked searchingly into her face.

"Oh! no, papa, I would never have dared to touch it. Please don't make me tell tales; but I know it wasn't Jim. Oh! *do* stop them quickly before they begin to whip him."

"Aunt Chloe," said Mr. Dinsmore, "go down to my father and tell him it is my request that the punishment should be delayed a few moments until I come down."

Then, taking Elsie's hand, he led her into her room again. "Now, my daughter, if you want to save Jim, it will be necessary for you to tell *all* you know about this affair," he said.

"I don't like to tell tales, papa," pleaded the little girl, "I think it so very mean. Is it not enough for me to tell that I know Jim didn't do it?"

"No, Elsie; I have already said that it is *quite necessary* for you to tell *all you know.*"

"O papa! don't make me; I don't like to do it," she urged with tears in her eyes.

"I should be very much ashamed of you and quite unwilling to own you as my child, if under any other circumstances you were willing to tell tales," he replied in a tone of kindness that quite surprised Elsie, "but," he added firmly, "it is the only way to save Jim; if you do not now make a full disclosure of all you know, he will be severely whipped and sent away to work on the plantation, which will distress his poor old mother exceedingly."

Her story was told with evident reluctance, but in a simple, straightforward manner that attested its truthfulness.

Mr. Dinsmore listened in silence, but with an expression of indignation on his handsome features; and the moment she had finished he rose and led her from the room.

"You must repeat this story to your grandfather," he said.

"O papa! must I? Won't you tell him? Please don't make me do it," she pleaded, trembling.

"My daughter, you *must*," he replied, so sternly that she dared not make any further resistance, but quietly submitted to be led into her grandfather's presence.

None of the other members of the family had left the room, and all wore an anxious, expectant look, as Mr. Dinsmore entered, leading Elsie by the hand.

"I have brought you another witness, sir," he said, "for it seems Elsie was present when the mischief was done."

"Ah!" exclaimed the old gentleman, "then I may hope to get at the truth. Elsie, who broke my watch?"

"It was not Jim, grandpa, indeed, *indeed*, it was not; but oh! *please* don't make me say who it was," replied the little girl beseechingly.

"Elsie!" exclaimed her father in a tone of stern reproof.

"O papa! how can I?" she sobbed, trembling and clinging to his hand as she caught a threatening look from Arthur.

"Come, come, child, you must tell us all you know about it," said her grandfather, "or else I can't let Jim off."

Mr. Dinsmore was looking down at his little girl, and, following the direction of her glance, perceived the cause of her terror. "Don't be afraid to speak out and tell all you know, daughter, for I will protect you," he said, pressing the little trembling hand in his and at the same time giving Arthur a meaning look.

"Yes, yes, speak out, child; speak out at once; no one shall hurt you for telling the truth," exclaimed her grandfather.

"I will, grandpa," she said, trembling and weeping, "but please don't be very angry with Arthur; if you will forgive him this time, I think he will never meddle any more; and I am quite sure he did not mean to break it."

"So it *was* you, after all, you young rascal! I knew it from the first!" cried the old gentleman, striding across the room, seizing the boy by the shoulder and shaking him roughly.

"But go on, Elsie, let us have the whole story," he added, turning to her again, but still keeping his hold upon Arthur. "You young dog!" he added, when she had finished. "Yes, I'll forgive you when you've had a good, sound flogging, and a week's solitary confinement on bread and water, but not before."

So saying, he was about to lead him from the room, when Elsie suddenly sprang forward, and with clasped hands, and flushed, eager face, she pleaded earnestly, beseechingly, "O grandpa! don't whip him, don't punish him! He will never be so naughty again. Will you, Arthur? Let *me pay* for the watch, grandpa, and don't punish him. I would so like to do it."

"It isn't the moneyed value of the watch I care for, child," replied the old gentleman, contemptuously. "But I will teach this young rascal to let my property alone," and with almost fierce determination, he tightened his grasp upon the boy's arm and dragged him from the room.

Chapter 6

Yea, though I walk through the valley of the shadow of death, I will fear no evil; for thou art with me; thy rod and thy staff, they comfort me.

—Psalms xxiii. 4

'Tis but the cruel artifice of fate,
Thus to refine and vary on our woes,
To raise us from despair and give us hopes,
Only to plunge us in the gulf again,
And make us doubly wretched.

—TRAP'S *Abramuh*

IT WAS Sabbath morning, and Elsie, ready dressed for church, stood in the portico waiting for her father to come down and lift her into the carriage in which Adelaide, Lora, and Enna were already seated.

The coachman was in his seat, and the horses, a pair of young and fiery steeds purchased by Mr. Dinsmore only a few days before, were impatiently stamping and tossing their heads.

"I don't exactly like the actions of those horses, Ajax," remarked Mr. Dinsmore, as he came out putting on his gloves, "I did not intend to have them put in harness to-day. Do you feel quite sure of being able to hold them in?" glancing uneasily first at the horses and then at Elsie.

"Ki! marster, dis here chile been able to hold in a'most anything," exclaimed the negro.

"Elsie," said her father, still looking a little uneasy in spite of Ajax's boasting, "I think it would be just as well for you to stay at home."

Elsie made no reply in words, but her answering look spoke such intense disappointment, such earnest entreaty, that, saying, "Ah! well, I suppose there is no real danger; and since you seem so anxious to go, I will not compel you to stay at home," he lifted her into the carriage, and, seating himself beside her, ordered the coachman to drive on as carefully as he could.

"Elsie, change seats with me," said Enna, "I want to sit beside Brother Horace."

"No," replied Mr. Dinsmore, laying his hand on his little daughter's shoulder, "Elsie's place is by me, and she shall sit nowhere else."

"Do you think we are in any danger of being run away with?" asked Adelaide, a little anxiously, as she observed him glancing once or twice out of the window, and was at the same time sensible that their motion was unusually rapid.

"The horses are young and fiery, but Ajax is an excellent driver," he replied evasively. "You may be sure that if I had thought the danger very great I would have left Elsie at home."

They reached the church without accident, but on their return the horses took fright while going down a hill and rushed along at a furious rate, which threatened every instant to upset the carriage.

Elsie thought they were going very fast, but did not know that there was real danger until her father suddenly lifted her from her seat, and, placing her between his knees, held her tightly, as though he feared she would be snatched from his grasp.

Elsie looked up into his face. It was deadly pale, and his eyes were fixed upon her with an expression of anguish.

"Dear papa," she whispered, "God will take care of us."

"I would give all I am worth to have you safe at home," he answered hoarsely, pressing her closer and closer to him.

Oh! even in that moment of fearful peril, when death seemed just at hand, those words and the affectionate clasp of her father's arm, sent a thrill of intense joy to the love-famished heart of the little girl.

But destruction seemed inevitable. Lora was leaning back, half fainting with terror, Adelaide scarcely less alarmed, while Enna clung to her, sobbing most bitterly.

Elsie alone preserved a cheerful serenity. Even death had no terrors to the simple, unquestioning faith of the little child who had put her trust in Jesus.

But they were not to perish thus; for at that moment a powerful negro, who was walking along the road, hearing an unusual sound, turned about, caught sight of the vehicle coming toward him at such a rapid rate, and, instantly comprehending the peril of the travelers, planted himself in the middle of the road, and, at the risk of life and limb, caught the horses by the bridle—the sudden and unexpected check throwing them upon their haunches, and bringing the carriage to an instant standstill.

"Thank God, we are saved! That fellow

shall be well rewarded for his brave deed," exclaimed Mr. Dinsmore, throwing open the carriage door.

Then, leaping to the ground, he lifted Elsie out, set her down, and gave his hand to his sisters one after the other.

They were almost at the entrance of the avenue, and all preferred to walk the short distance to the house rather than again trust themselves to the horses.

Mr. Dinsmore lingered a moment to speak to the man who had done them such good service, and to give some directions to the coachman; and then, taking the hand of his little girl, who had been waiting for him, he walked slowly on, neither of them speaking a word until they reached the house, when he stooped and kissed her cheek, asking very kindly if she had recovered from her fright.

"Yes, papa," she answered in a quiet tone, "I knew that God would take care of us. Oh! wasn't He good to keep us all from being killed?"

"Yes," he said very gravely. "Go, now, and let mammy get you ready for dinner."

As Elsie was sitting alone in her room that

afternoon she was surprised by a visit from
Lora; it being very seldom that the elder girls
cared to enter her apartment.

Lora looked a little pale, and more grave
and thoughtful than Elsie had ever seen her.
For a while she sat in silence, then suddenly
burst out, "Oh, Elsie! I can't help thinking
all the time, what if we had been killed! where
would we all be now? where would *I* have
been? I believe *you* would have gone straight
to heaven, Elsie; but *I*—oh! I should have been
with the rich man the minister read about this
morning, lifting up my eyes in torment."

And Lora covered her face with her hands
and shuddered.

Presently she went on again. "I was terribly frightened, and so were the rest—all but
you, Elsie; tell me, *do*—what kept *you* from
being afraid?"

"I was thinking," said Elsie gently, turning
over the leaves of her little Bible as she spoke,
"of this sweet verse: 'Yea, though I walk
through the valley of the shadow of death, I
will fear no evil; for thou art with me'; and oh,
Lora! it made me so happy to think that Jesus
was there with me, and that if I were killed,

I should only fall asleep to wake up again in His arms; then how could I be afraid?"

"Ah! I would give anything to feel as you do," said Lora, sighing. "But tell me, Elsie, did you not feel afraid for the rest of us?"

"It all passed so quickly, you know, Lora, almost in a moment," she said, "so that I only had time to think of papa and myself; and I have prayed so much for him that I felt quite sure God would spare him until he should be prepared to die. It was very selfish, I know," she added, with deep humility, "but it was only for a moment, and I can't tell you how thankful I was for *all* our spared lives."

"Don't look so—as if you had done something very wicked, Elsie," replied Lora, sighing again. "I'm sure we have given you little enough reason to care whatever becomes of us; but oh! Elsie, if you can only tell me how to be a Christian, I mean now to try very hard; indeed, I am determined never to rest until I am one."

"Oh, Lora, how glad I am!" cried Elsie, joyfully, "for I know that if you are really in earnest, you will succeed; for no one ever yet failed who tried aright. Jesus said, '*Every one* that asketh, receiveth; and he that seeketh, findeth; and to him that knocketh, it *shall* be opened.' Is not *that* encouraging?"

"Yes," said Lora, "but you have not answered my question: *how* am I to seek? that is, what means am I to use to get rid of my sins, and get a new heart? how make myself pleasing in the sight of God? what must I *do* to be saved?"

"Do, Lora! *Only believe,*" replied Elsie in the same earnest tone. "Jesus has done and suffered all that is necessary; and now we have nothing at all to do but go to Him and be washed in that fountain; believe Him when He says, 'I *give* unto them eternal life'; just accept the gift, and trust and love Him."

"But surely, Elsie, I *can,* I *must do something.*"

"Yes, God tells us to repent; and He says, 'Give me thine heart'; you can do that; you can love Jesus; at least He will enable you to, if you ask Him, and He will teach you to be sorry for your sins. Jesus said, 'Your Heavenly Father is more willing to give His Holy Spirit to them that ask Him, than parents are to give good gifts unto their children.'

Oh, Lora! don't be afraid to ask for it. But remember that you must come very humbly; feeling that you are a great sinner, and not worthy to be heard, and only hoping to be forgiven, because Jesus died. The Bible says, 'God resisteth the proud, but giveth grace unto the humble.' "

Lora lingered the greater part of the afternoon in Elsie's room, asking her questions, or listening to her while she read the Scriptures, or repeated some beautiful hymn, or spoke in her sweet, childish way of her own peace and joy in believing in Jesus.

Chapter 7

The smallest worm will turn, being trodden on.
—SHAKESPEARE, *Richard III*

A blossom full of promise is life's joy,
That never comes to fruit. Hope, for a time,
Suns the young flow'ret in its gladsome light,
And it looks flourishing—a little while—
'Tis pass'd, we know not whither, but 'tis gone.
—MISS LANDON

IT WAS Miss Day's custom to present to the parents of her pupils a monthly report of their conduct and recitations. The regular time for this had occurred once since Mr. Horace Dinsmore's return, when she, of course, handed Elsie's to him.

It was now time for a second report; but the past month had been a most unfortunate one for the little girl; so much were her thoughts occupied with the longing desire to gain her father's love, so depressed were her spirits by her constant failure to do so, that she often found it impossible to give her mind to her lessons.

Arthur, too, during much of the time before and since the week of his imprisonment, had been more than usually annoying, shaking her chair and jogging her elbow so frequently when she was writing, that her copybook presented by no means so good an appearance as usual; and never had Miss Day made out so poor a report for her. She carried it with much secret satisfaction to the little girl's father and entered a long complaint of the child's idleness and inattention.

"Send her to me," he said angrily. "She will find me in my own room."

Miss Day had left Elsie in the schoolroom putting her desk in order after the day's work and she found her still there on her return.

"Elsie," said she with a malicious smile, "your father wishes to see you immediately. He is in his room."

The child turned red and pale by turns and trembled so violently that for a moment she was quite unable to move.

"I advise you to go at once," said Miss Day, "for no doubt the longer you wait the worse it will be for you."

At the same moment Mr. Dinsmore's voice was heard calling in a stern, angry tone, "Elsie!"

Making a violent effort to control her feelings, she started up and hastened to obey.

The door of his room stood open, and she walked in, asking in a trembling voice, "Did you call me, papa?"

"Yes," said he, "I did. Come here to me!"

He was sitting with the copybook and report in his hand, and there was much severity in both tone and look as he addressed her.

"Can you tell me, Elsie, how it happens that your teacher brings me so bad a report of your conduct and lessons during the past month? She says you have been very idle; and the report tells the same story; and this copybook presents a shameful appearance."

The child answered only by tears and sobs.

"Elsie," he said, sternly, "when I ask a question, I require an answer instantly."

"O papa!" she answered pleadingly, "I couldn't study. I'm very sorry—I'll try to do better—only don't be very angry with me."

"I am very angry with you; very angry, indeed," said he in the same severe tone, "and very strongly inclined to punish you. You *couldn't* study, eh? What reason can you assign, pray? Were you not well?"

"I don't know, sir," sobbed the little girl.

"You don't *know*? Very well, then, I think you could not be very ill without knowing it, and so you seem to have no excuse at all to offer? However, I will not inflict any punishment upon you *this* time, as you seem to be really sorry and have promised to do better; but I warn you that unless your next copybook presents a better appearance than this, I certainly shall punish you.

"There are a number of pages here that look quite well," he continued, turning over the leaves. "That shows what you *can* do, if you choose. Hush!" as Elsie seemed about to speak, "not a word. You may go now." And throwing himself back in his easy chair, he took up a newspaper and began to read.

With a sinking heart Elsie turned away and sought the solitude of her own room, there to weep, and mourn, and pray that she might one day possess the love she so pined for, and bitterly to reproach herself for having by the failures of the past month put it farther from her.

And soon a thought came to her which added greatly to her distress. If Arthur continued his persecutions, how could she make the next copybook more presentable? And in case it were not, her father had said positively that he would punish her; and oh! how could she bear punishment from him, when a word or look of displeasure almost broke her heart?

She saw no escape from the dreaded punishment, unless she could persuade Arthur to cease his annoyances; and of that there was little hope.

But she carried her trouble to her Heavenly Father, and asked Him to help her. She was still on her knees, when someone knocked at the door.

She opened it to find her Aunt Adelaide standing there.

"Elsie," she said, "I am writing to Miss Rose; have you any word to send? You may write a little note, if you choose, and I will enclose it in my letter. But what is the matter, child?" she suddenly exclaimed, kindly taking the little girl's hand in hers.

With many tears and sobs Elsie told her the whole story, not omitting her papa's threat, and her fear that she could not, on account of Arthur's persecutions, avoid the punishment.

Adelaide's sympathies were enlisted, and she drew the sobbing child to her side, saying, as she pressed a kiss on her cheek: "Never mind, Elsie, I will take my book or needlework to the schoolroom every day and sit there during the writing hour."

When her Aunt Adelaide left her, Elsie went to her bureau, and unlocking a drawer, took out a purse she was knitting for her father, to replace the one she had given to Miss Allison.

She had commenced it before his return, and having spent upon it nearly every spare moment since, when she could feel secure from intrusion, she now had it nearly completed.

She had been much comforted and encouraged by her aunt's sympathy and kind promise of assistance, and, though there were still traces of tears upon it, the little face looked quite bright and cheerful again as she settled herself in her little sewing chair, and began her work.

"Mammy, is papa in his room?" asked Elsie as she put the finishing touches to the purse.

"No, darlin', Marster Horace he rode out wid de strange gentlemen an hour ago."

Elsie laid her needles away in her work-basket, and opening her writing desk, selected a bit of note paper, on which she wrote in her very best hand: "A present for my dear papa, from his little daughter Elsie!" This she carefully pinned to the purse, and then carried it to her papa's room, intending to leave it on his toilet table.

Fearing that he might possibly have returned, she knocked gently at the door, but receiving no answer, opened it and went in; but she had not gone more than halfway across the room when she heard his voice behind her, asking in a tone of mingled surprise and displeasure, "What are you doing in my room in my absence, Elsie?"

She started and turned round, pale and trembling, and lifting her eyes pleadingly to his face, silently placed the purse in his hand.

"I made it for you, dear papa," she said in a low, tremulous tone, "do please take it."

"It is really very pretty," he said, examining it. "Is it possible it is your work? I had no idea you had so much taste and skill. Thank you, daughter, I shall take it and use it with a great deal of pleasure."

Fearing he might possibly have returned,
she knocked gently at the door.

He took her hand as he spoke, and sitting down, lifted her to his knee, saying, "Elsie, my child, why do you always seem so afraid of me? I don't like it."

With a sudden impulse she threw her arms around his neck and pressed her lips to his cheek; then dropping her head on his breast, she sobbed: "O papa! *dear* papa, I *do love* you so *very* dearly! will you not love me? O papa! love me a *little*. I know I've been naughty very often, but I will *try* to be good."

Then for the first time he folded her in his arms and kissed her tenderly, saying in a moved tone, "I *do* love you, my darling, my own little daughter."

Oh! the words were sweeter to Elsie's ear than the most delicious music! her joy was too great for words, for anything but tears.

"Why do you cry so, my darling?" he asked soothingly, stroking her hair and kissing her again and again.

"O papa! because I am so happy, so *very* happy," she sobbed.

"Do you indeed care so very much for my love?" he asked. "Then, my daughter, you must not tremble and turn pale whenever I speak to you, as though I were a cruel tyrant."

"O papa! I cannot help it, when you look and speak so sternly. I love you so dearly I cannot bear to have you angry with me; but I'm not afraid of you now."

"That is right," he said, caressing her again. "But there is the tea bell," he added, setting her down. "Go into the dressing room there, and bathe your eyes, and then come to me."

She hastened to do his bidding, and then taking her hand, he led her down and seated her in her usual place by his side.

Everything now went on very pleasantly for some days. Elsie did not see a great deal of her father, as he was frequently away from home for a day or two, and when he returned, generally brought a number of visitors with him; but whenever he did notice her it was very kindly, and she was gradually overcoming the fear of him, and constantly hoping that the time would soon come when he would have more leisure to bestow upon her. She was happy now, and with a mind at ease, was able to learn her lessons well; and as Aunt Adelaide faithfully kept her promise and thus freed her from Arthur's annoyances, she was enabled to do justice to her writing. She took great pains, her copybook showed a marked improvement in her penmanship, and its pages had not yet been defaced by a single blot, so that she was looking forward with pleasing anticipations to the time when her report should again be presented to her father.

Chapter 8

He that pursues an act that is attended
With doubtful issues, for the means, had need
Of policy and force to make it speed.
          —T. NABB'S *Unfortunate Mother*

Joy never feasts so high,
As when the first course is of misery.
          —SUCKLING'S *Aglaura*

IT WAS Friday, and the next morning was the time when the reports were to be presented. School had closed, and all but Elsie had already left the room, but she was carefully arranging the books in her desk.

When she had quite finished her work she took up her report book and glanced over it. As her eye rested for an instant upon the one bad mark, she sighed a little and murmured to herself, "I am *so* sorry; I wish papa knew how little I really deserved it." It had been given her one unfortunate morning when Miss Day had been unreasonable to the last degree and Elsie as usual had been the principal sufferer from her ill humor.

Then, laying it aside, she opened her copybook and turned over the leaves with unalloyed pleasure, for not one of its pages was defaced by a single blot, and from beginning to end it gave evidence of painstaking carefulness and decided improvement.

"Ah! surely *this will please dear papa!*" she exclaimed, half aloud. "How good Aunt Adelaide was to sit here with me!"

Then, putting it carefully in its place, she closed and locked the desk, and carrying the key to her room, laid it on the mantel, where she was in the habit of keeping it.

Now it so happened that afternoon that Arthur, who had made himself sick by over-indulgence in sweetmeats, remained at home while all the rest of the family were out, walking, riding, or visiting.

He was not usually very fond of reading, but while lying on the lounge in the nursery, it suddenly occurred to him that he would like to look at a book he had seen Elsie reading that morning.

Elsie, he knew, was out, and Chloe in the kitchen; so, feeling certain there would be no one to interfere with him, he went directly to the little girl's room to look for the book. He soon found it lying on the mantel; but the desk key lay right beside it, and as he caught sight of that he gave a half scream of delight, for he guessed at once to what lock it belonged, and felt that he now could accomplish the revenge he had plotted ever since the affair of the watch.

He put out his hand to take it, but drew it back again, and stood for a moment balancing in his mind the chances of detection.

He decided to run the risk, and laying down the book, he took the key, went to the door, looked carefully up and down the hall to make sure of not being seen by any of the servants, and having satisfied himself on that point, hurried to the schoolroom. His work did not take long, however, and he hurried back to Elsie's room, put the key just where he had found it, and taking the book, returned to the nursery without having met anyone.

He threw himself down on a couch and tried to read. He kept the book until Elsie came in search of it.

He looked very guilty as the little girl came in, but not seeming to notice it, she merely said: "I am looking for my book. I thought perhaps someone might have brought it in here. Oh! *you* have it, Arthur! well, keep it, if you wish; I can read it just as well another time."

"Here, take it," said he roughly, pushing it toward her, "I don't want it; 'tisn't a bit pretty."

"Young ladies and gentlemen," said the governess, as they were about closing their exercises the next morning, "this is the regular day for the reports, and they are all made out. Miss Elsie, here is yours; bring your copybook and carry both to your papa."

Elsie obeyed, not without some trembling, yet hoping, as there was but *one* bad mark in the report and the copybook showed such evident marks of care and painstaking, her papa would not be very seriously displeased.

It being the last day of the term, the exercises of the morning had varied somewhat from the usual routine, and the writing hour had been entirely omitted; thus it happened that Elsie had not opened her copybook.

She found her father in his room. He took the report first from her hand, and glancing over it, said with a slight frown: "I see you have one *very* bad mark for recitation; but as there is only one, and the others are remarkably good, I will excuse it."

Then taking the copybook and opening it, much to Elsie's surprise and alarm, he gave her a glance of great displeasure, turned rapidly over the leaves, then laying it down, said in his sternest tones, "I see I shall have to keep my promise, Elsie."

"What, papa?" she asked, turning pale.

"*What!*" said he, "do you ask me what? Did I not tell you *positively* that I would *punish* you if your copybook this month did not present a better appearance than it did last?"

"O papa! does it not? I tried so very hard; and there are no blots in it."

"No blots?" said he, "what do you call these?" and he turned over the leaves again, holding the book so that she could see that almost every one was blotted in several places.

Elsie gazed at them in astonishment; then, looking up into his face, she said earnestly but fearfully, "Papa, I did not do it."

"Who did then?" he asked.

"Indeed, papa, I do not know," she replied.

"I must inquire into this business," he said, rising, "and if it is not your fault you shall not be punished; but if I find you have been telling me a falsehood, Elsie, I shall punish you much more severely than if you had not denied your fault."

And taking her by the hand as he spoke, he led her back to the schoolroom.

"Miss Day," said he, showing the book, "Elsie says these blots are not her work; can you tell me whose they are?"

"Miss Elsie *generally* tells the truth, sir," replied Miss Day sarcastically, "but I must say that in this instance I think she has failed, as her desk has a good lock, and she herself keeps the key."

"Elsie," he asked, "is this so?"

"Yes, papa."

"And have you ever left your desk unlocked, or the key lying about?"

"No, papa; I am quite certain I have not," she answered unhesitatingly, though her voice trembled, and she grew very pale.

"Very well, then *I* am quite certain you have told me a falsehood, since it is evident this *must* have been your work. Elsie, I can forgive anything but falsehood, but that I *never will* forgive. Come with me. I shall teach you to speak the truth to *me* at least, if to no one else," and taking her hand again, he dragged her from the room, for he was terribly angry, his face fairly pale with passion.

Lora came in while he was speaking, and, certain that *Elsie* would never be caught in a falsehood, her eye quickly sought Arthur's.

He was sitting there with a very guilty countenance.

She hastily crossed the room, and, speaking in a low tone, said, "Arthur, *you* have had a hand in this business I know; now confess it quickly, or Horace will half kill Elsie."

"You don't know anything about it," said he doggedly.

"Yes, I do," she answered, "and if you do not speak out at once, *I* shall save Elsie, and find means to prove your guilt afterwards; so you had much better confess."

"Go away," he exclaimed angrily, "I have nothing to confess."

Seeing it was useless to try to move him, Lora turned away and hurried to Horace's room, which, in her haste, she entered without knocking, he having fortunately neglected to fasten the door. She was just in time: he

had a small riding whip in his hand, and Elsie
stood beside him, pale as death, too much
frightened even to cry, and trembling so that
she could scarcely stand.

He turned an angry glance on his sister as
she entered; but taking no notice of it, she
exclaimed eagerly: "Horace, don't punish
Elsie, for I am certain she is innocent."

He laid down the whip, asking, "*How* do
you know it? What *proof* have you? I shall
be very glad to be convinced," he added, his
countenance relaxing somewhat in its stern
and angry expression.

"I am sure Arthur is at the bottom of this,
for, though he will not acknowledge, he does
not deny it. And now I recollect, I saw and
examined Elsie's book only yesterday, and it
was then quite free from blots."

A great change had come over her brother's
countenance while she was speaking.

"Thank you, Lora," he said cordially, as
soon as she had done, "you have quite convinced me, and saved me from punishing Elsie
as unjustly as severely. That last assurance
I consider quite sufficient of itself to establish
her innocence."

Lora turned and went out feeling very happy, and as she closed the door, Elsie's papa took her in his arms, saying, in loving, tender tones: "My poor little daughter; my own darling child! I have been cruelly unjust to you, have I not?"

"Dear papa, you thought I deserved it," she said, throwing her arms around his neck and laying her head on his breast.

"Do you love me, Elsie, dearest?" he asked, folding her closer to his heart.

"So very, *very* much. O papa! if you would only love me!" The last word was almost a sob.

"I do, my darling, my own precious child," he said, caressing her again and again. "I do love my little girl, and I am more thankful than words can express that I have been saved from punishing her unjustly. I could never forgive myself if I had done it. I would rather have lost half I am worth; also I fear it would have turned all her love for me into hatred, and justly, too."

"No, papa, oh! no, *no; nothing* could ever do that!" and the little arms were clasped closer and closer about his neck.

"There, there, daughter! don't cry any more;

we will try to forget all about it, and talk of
something else," he said soothingly.

Mr. Dinsmore sat there a long time with his
little daughter on his knee, caressing her more
tenderly than ever before; and Elsie was very
happy, and talked more freely to him than she
had ever done, telling him of her joys and her
sorrows; how dearly she had loved Miss Allison—what happy hours they had spent together in studying the Bible and in prayer—
how grieved she was when her friend went
away—and how intensely she enjoyed the
little letter now and then received from her;
and he listened to it all, apparently both
pleased and interested, encouraging her to go
on by an occasional question or a word of assent or approval.

"What is this, Elsie?" he asked, taking hold
of the chain she always wore around her neck,
and drawing the miniature from her bosom.

As he touched the spring and the case flew
open, revealing the sweet, girlish face, it
needed not Elsie's low murmured "Mamma"
to tell him who that lovely lady was.

He gazed upon it with emotion, carried back
in memory to the time when for a few short

months she had been his own most cherished treasure. Then, looking from it to his child, he murmured, "Yes, she is very like—the same features, the same expression, complexion, hair and all—will be the very counterpart of her if she lives."

"Dear papa, am I like mamma?" asked Elsie, who had caught a part of his words.

"Yes, darling, very much indeed, and I hope you will grow more so."

"You loved mamma?" she said inquiringly.

"Dearly, *very* dearly."

"O papa! *tell* me about her! *do,* dear papa," she pleaded.

"I have not much to tell," he said, sighing. "I knew her only for a few short months before we were separated, never to meet again on earth."

"But we may hope to meet her in heaven, dear papa," said Elsie softly, "for she loved Jesus, and if we love Him we shall go there too when we die. Do you love Jesus, papa?" she timidly inquired, for she had seen him do a number of things which she knew to be wrong —such as riding out for pleasure on the Sabbath, reading secular newspapers, and engaging in worldly conversation—and she greatly feared he did not.

But instead of answering her question, he asked, "Do you, Elsie?"

"Oh! yes, sir; very, *very* much; even better than I love you, my own dear papa."

"How do you know?" he asked, looking keenly into her face.

"Just as I know that I love you, papa, or anyone else," she replied, lifting her eyes to his face in evident surprise at the strangeness of the question. "Ah, papa," she added, in her own sweet, simple way, "I do so love to talk of Jesus; to tell Him all my troubles, and ask Him to forgive my sins and make me holy; and then it is so sweet to know that He loves me, and will *always* love me, even if no one else does."

He kissed Elsie and set her down, saying, "Go now, my daughter, and prepare for dinner; it is almost time for the bell."

"You are not displeased, papa?" she inquired, looking up anxiously into his face.

"No, darling, not at all," he replied, stroking her hair. "Shall I ride with my little girl this afternoon?"

"Oh, papa! do you really mean it? I shall be so glad!" she exclaimed joyfully.

"Very well, then," he said, "it is settled. But go now; there is the bell. No, stay!" he added quickly, as she turned to obey, "think a moment and tell me where you put the key of your desk yesterday, for it must have been then the mischief was done. Had you it with you when you rode out?"

Suddenly Elsie's face flushed, and she exclaimed eagerly, "Ah! I remember now! I left it on the mantelpiece, papa, and——"

But here she paused, as if sorry she had said so much.

"And what?" he asked.

"I think I had better not say it, papa! I'm afraid I *ought* not, for I don't really *know,* and it seems so wrong to suspect people."

"You need not express any suspicions," said her father, "I do not wish you to do so; but I must insist upon having all the facts you can furnish me with. Was Aunt Chloe in your room all the time you were away?"

"No, sir; she told me she went down to the kitchen directly after I left, and did not come up again until after I returned."

"Very well; do you know whether anyone else entered the room during your absence?"

"I do not *know,* papa, but I *think* Arthur must have been in, because when I came home I found him reading a book which I had left lying on the mantelpiece," she answered in a low, reluctant tone.

"Ah, ha! that is just it! I see it all now," he exclaimed with a satisfied nod. "There, that will do, Elsie; go now and make haste down to your dinner."

But Elsie lingered, and, in answer to a look of kind inquiry from her father, said coaxingly, "Please, papa, don't be very angry with him. I think he did not know how much I cared about my book."

"You are very forgiving, Elsie; but go, child, I shall not abuse him," Mr. Dinsmore answered with an imperative gesture, and the little girl hurried from the room.

It happened that just at this time the elder Mr. Dinsmore and his wife were paying a visit to some friends in the city, and thus Elsie's papa had been left head of the house for the time. Arthur, knowing this to be the state of affairs, and that though his father was expected to return that evening, his mother would be absent for some days, was beginning to be a good deal fearful of the consequences of his misconduct, and not without reason, for his brother's wrath was now fully aroused, and he was determined that the boy should not on this occasion escape the penalty of his misdeeds.

Arthur was already in the dining room when Mr. Dinsmore came down.

"Arthur," said he, "I wish you to step into the library a moment; I have something to say to you."

"I don't want to hear it," muttered the boy.

"I dare say not, sir; but that makes no difference," replied his brother. "Walk into the library at once."

Arthur returned a scowl of defiance, muttering almost under his breath, "I'll do as I please about that"; but cowed by his brother's determined look and manner, he slowly and reluctantly obeyed.

"Now, sir," said Mr. Dinsmore, when he had him fairly in the room and had closed the door behind them, "I wish to know how you came to meddle with Elsie's copybook."

"I didn't," was the angry rejoinder.

"Take care, sir; I know all about it," said Mr. Dinsmore in a warning tone, "it is useless for you to deny it. Yesterday, while Elsie was out and Aunt Chloe in the kitchen, you went to her room, took the key of her desk from the mantelpiece where she had left it, went to the schoolroom and did the mischief, hoping to get her into trouble thereby, and then relocking the desk and returning the key to its proper place, thought you had escaped detection; and I was very near giving my poor, innocent little girl the whipping you so richly deserve."

Arthur looked up in astonishment.

"Who told you?" he asked, "nobody saw me"; then, catching himself, said hastily, "I tell you I didn't do it. I don't know anything about it."

"Will you dare to tell me such a falsehood as that again?" exclaimed Mr. Dinsmore angrily, taking him by the collar and shaking him roughly.

"Let me alone now," whined the culprit. "I want my dinner, I say."

"You'll get no dinner to-day, I can tell you," replied his brother. "I am going to lock you

*Mr. Dinsmore took him by the collar
and shook him roughly.*

into your bedroom and keep you there until your father comes home; and then if *he* doesn't give you the flogging you deserve, *I* will; for I intend you shall have your deserts for once in your life. I know that all this is in revenge for Elsie's forced testimony in the affair of the watch, and I gave you fair warning then that I would see to it that any attempt to abuse my child should receive its just reward."

He took the boy by the arm as he spoke, to lead him from the room.

Mr. Horace Dinsmore had almost unbounded influence over his father, who was very proud of him; the old gentleman also utterly despised everything mean and underhanded, and upon being made acquainted by Horace with Arthur's misdemeanors he inflicted upon him as severe a punishment as anyone could have desired.

Chapter 9

Keep the Sabbath day to sanctify it, as the Lord thy
God hath commanded thee.—Deuteronomy v. 12

> She is mine own;
> And I as rich in having such a jewel
> As twenty seas, if all their sand were pearl,
> The water nectar, and the rocks pure gold.
> —SHAKESPEARE, *Two Gentlemen of Verona*

AND now happy days had come to the little
Elsie. Her father treated her with the tenderest affection, and kept her with him almost
constantly, seeming scarcely willing to have
her out of his sight for an hour. He took her
with him wherever he went in his rides and
walks and visits to the neighboring planters.

He helped her with all her studies, taught
her something of botany and geology in their
walks, helped her to see and correct the faults
of her drawing, sang with her when she played,
bought her quantities of new music, and engaged the best masters to instruct her—in
short, took a lively interest in all her pursuits
and pleasures, gave her every indulgence, and
lavished upon her the tenderest caresses. He

was very proud of her beauty, her sweetness, her intelligence, and talent; and nothing pleased him better than to hear them spoken of by others in terms of praise.

And Elsie was very happy; the soft eyes grew bright with happiness, and the little face lost its pensive expression, and became as round, rosy and merry as Enna's.

Miss Day went North, expecting to be absent several months, and during the school vacation Elsie's papa took her traveling, spending some time at different watering places. It was her first journey since she had been old enough to care for such things and she enjoyed it exceedingly. They left home in July, and did not return until September.

"How bright and happy the child looks!" was Adelaide's remark on the day of their return.

"Yes," said Lora, "and how entirely she seems to have overcome her fear of Horace!"

Yes, Elsie had lost her fear of her father, and could now talk to him, and tell him her feelings and wishes, as freely as ever Enna did; and no wonder, for in all these weeks he had never given her one harsh word or look; but indeed he had had no occasion to do so, for she was always docile and obedient.

It was a Sabbath afternoon. Quite a number of guests had dined at Roselands. They were nearly all gentlemen, and were collected in the drawing room, laughing, jesting, talking politics, and conversing with each other and the ladies upon various worldly topics, apparently quite forgetful that it was the Lord's day, which He has commanded to be kept holy in thought and word, as well as deed.

"May I ask what you are in search of, Mr. Eversham?" inquired Adelaide, as she noticed one of the guests glance around the room with a rather disappointed air.

"Yes, Miss Adelaide; I was looking for little Miss Elsie. Travilla has given me so very glowing an account of her precocious musical talent that I have conceived a great desire to hear her play and sing."

"Do you hear that, Horace?" asked Adelaide, turning to her brother.

"Yes, and I shall be most happy to gratify you, Eversham," replied the young father with a proud smile.

He crossed the room to summon a servant,

but as he placed his hand upon the bell rope, Mrs. Dinsmore arrested his movement.

"Stay, Horace," she said, "you had better not send for her."

"May I be permitted to ask *why,* madam?" he inquired in a tone of mingled surprise and annoyance.

"Because she will not sing," answered the lady coolly.

"Pardon me, madam, but I think she will, if *I bid* her to do it," he said with flashing eyes.

"No, she will not," persisted Mrs. Dinsmore in the same cold, quiet tone. "She will tell you she is wiser than her father, and that it would be a sin to obey him in this. Believe me, she will most assuredly defy your authority; so you had better take my advice and let her alone—thus sparing yourself the mortification of exhibiting before your guests your inability to govern your child."

Mr. Dinsmore bit his lip with vexation.

"Thank you," he said haughtily, "but I prefer convincing you that that inability lies wholly in your own imagination; and I am quite at a loss to understand upon what you found your opinion, as Elsie has never yet made the very slightest resistance to my authority."

He had given the bell rope a vigorous pull while speaking, and a servant now appearing in answer to the summons, he sent him with a message to Elsie, requiring her presence in the drawing room.

Then turning away from his stepmother, who looked after him with a gleam of triumph in her eye, he joined the group of gentlemen already gathered about the piano, where Adelaide had just taken her seat and begun a brilliant overture.

Yet, outwardly calm and self-satisfied as his demeanor may have been, Horace Dinsmore was even now regretting the step he had just taken; for remembering Elsie's conscientious scruples regarding the observance of the Sabbath—which he had for the moment forgotten—he foresaw that there would be a struggle, probably a severe one; and though, having always found her docile and yielding, he felt no doubt of the final result, he would willingly have avoided the contest, could he have done so without a sacrifice of pride; but, as he said to himself, with a slight sigh, he had now gone too far to retreat; and then he had all along felt that this struggle must come *some* time, and perhaps it was as well *now* as at any other.

Elsie was alone in her room, spending the Sabbath afternoon in her usual manner, when the servant came to say that her papa wished to see her in the drawing room. The little girl was a good deal alarmed at the summons, for the thought instantly flashed upon her, "He is going to bid me play and sing, or do something else which it is not right to do on the Sabbath day."

But remembering that he never had done so, she hoped he might not now; yet before she obeyed the call she knelt down for a moment, and prayed earnestly for strength to do right, however difficult it might be.

"Come here, daughter," her father said, as she entered the room. He spoke in his usual pleasant, affectionate tone, yet Elsie started, trembled, and turned pale; for catching sight of the group at the piano, and her Aunt Adelaide just vacating the music stool, she at once perceived what was in store for her.

"Here, Elsie," said her father, selecting a song which she had learned during their absence and sang remarkably well, "I wish you to sing this for my friends; they are anxious to hear it."

"Will not to-morrow do, papa?" she asked in a low, tremulous tone.

Mrs. Dinsmore, who had drawn near to listen, now looked at Horace with a meaning smile, which he affected not to see.

"Certainly not, Elsie," he said, "we want it now. You know it quite well enough without any more practice."

"I did not want to wait for *that* reason, papa," she replied in the same low, trembling tones, "but you know, this is the holy Sabbath day."

"Well, my daughter, and what of that? I consider this song perfectly proper to be sung to-day, and that ought to satisfy you that you will not be doing wrong to sing it; remember what I said to you some weeks ago; and now sit down and sing it at once."

"O papa! I *cannot* sing it to-day; *please* let me wait until to-morrow."

"Elsie," he said in his sternest tones, "sit down to the piano instantly, and do as I bid you, and let me hear no more of this nonsense."

She sat down, but raising her pleading eyes, brimful of tears, to his face, she repeated her refusal. "Dear papa, I *cannot* sing it to-day, I *cannot* break the Sabbath."

"Elsie, you *must* sing it," said he, placing the music before her. "I have told you that it will not be breaking the Sabbath, and that is sufficient; you must let me judge for you in these matters."

"Let her wait until to-morrow, Dinsmore; to-morrow will suit us quite as well," urged several of the gentlemen, while Adelaide good-naturedly said, "Let me play it, Horace; I have no such scruples."

"No," he replied, "when I give my child a command, it is to be obeyed; I have *said* she should play it, and play it she *must;* she is not to suppose that she may set up her opinion of right and wrong against mine."

Elsie sat with her little hands folded in her lap, the tears streaming from her downcast eyes over her pale cheeks. She was trembling, but though there was no stubbornness in her countenance, the expression meek and humble, she made no movement toward obeying her father's order

There was a moment of silent waiting; then he said in his severest tone, "Elsie, you shall sit there till you obey me, though it should be until to-morrow morning."

"Yes, papa," she replied in a scarcely audible voice, and they all turned away and left her.

"You see now that you had better have taken my advice, Horace," remarked Mrs. Dinsmore in a triumphant tone. "I knew very well how it would end."

"Excuse me," said he, "but it has *not* ended; and before it does, I think she will learn that she has a stronger will than her own to deal with."

Elsie's position was a most uncomfortable one; her seat high and uneasy, and seeming to grow more and more so as the weary moments passed slowly away. No one came near her or seemed to notice her, yet she could hear them conversing in other parts of the room, and knew that they were sometimes looking at her, and, timid and bashful as she was, it seemed hard to bear. Then, too, her little heart was very sad as she thought of her father's displeasure, and feared that he would withdraw from her the affection which had been for the last few months the very sunshine of her life. Besides all this, the excitement of her feelings and the close and sultry air—for it was a very warm day—had brought on a nervous headache. She leaned forward and rested her head against the instrument, feeling in momentary danger of falling from her seat.

Thus two long hours had passed when Mr. Travilla came to her side, and said in a compassionate tone, "I am really very sorry for you, my little friend; but I advise you to submit to your papa. I see you are getting very weary sitting there, and I warn you not to hope to conquer him. I have known him for years, and a more determined person I never saw. Had you not better sing the song?—it will not take five minutes, and then your trouble will be all over."

Elsie raised her head and answered gently, "Thank you for your sympathy, Mr. Travilla, you are very kind; but I could not do it, because Jesus says, 'He that loveth father or mother more than me, is not worthy of me'; and I cannot disobey Him, even to please my own dear papa."

"But, Miss Elsie, why do you think it would be disobeying Him? Does the Bible say you must not sing songs on Sunday?"

"Mr. Travilla, it says the Sabbath is to be kept holy unto the Lord; that we are not to think our own thoughts, nor speak our own words, nor do our own actions; but all the day must be spent in studying God's word, or worshipping and praising Him, and there is no praise in that song—not one word about God or heaven."

"That is very true, Elsie, but still it is such a very little thing that I cannot think there would be much harm in it, or that God would be very angry with you for doing it."

"O Mr. Travilla!" she said, looking up at him in great surprise, "surely you know that there is no such thing as a *little sin;* and don't you remember about the man who picked up sticks on the Sabbath day?"

"No; what was it?"

"God commanded that he should be stoned to death, and it was done. Would you not have thought *that* a very little thing, Mr. Travilla?"

"Yes, I believe I should," said he, turning away with a very grave face.

"Dinsmore," he said, going up to his friend, "I am sure that child is conscientious; had you not better give up to her in this instance?"

"*Never,* Travilla," he answered with stern decision. "This is the first time she has rebelled against my authority, and if I let her conquer now, she will think she is always to have her own way. No; cost what it may, I *must* subdue her; she will have to learn that my will is law."

"Right, Horace," said the elder Mr. Dinsmore approvingly, "let her understand from the first that you are to be master; it is always the best plan."

"Excuse me, Dinsmore," said Travilla, "but I must say that I think a parent has no right to coerce a child into doing violence to its conscience."

"Nonsense!" replied his friend, a little angrily. "Elsie is entirely too young to set up her opinion against mine; she must allow me to judge for her in these matters for some years to come."

Another hour passed slowly away, and then the tea bell rang.

"Elsie," asked her father, coming to her

side, "are you ready to obey me now? If so, we will wait a moment to hear the song, and then you can go to your tea with us."

"Dear papa, I cannot break the Sabbath," she replied without lifting her head.

"Very well, then, I cannot break my word; you must sit there until you will submit; and until then you must fast. You are not only making yourself miserable by your disobedience and obstinacy, Elsie, but are mortifying and grieving *me* very much," he added in a subdued tone, as he turned away and left her.

The evening passed wearily away to the little girl; the drawing room was but dimly lighted, for the company had all deserted it to wander about the grounds, or sit on the portico enjoying the moonlight and the pleasant evening breeze, and the air indoors seemed insupportably close and sultry. At times Elsie could scarcely breathe, and she longed intensely to get out into the open air; every moment her seat grew more uncomfortable and the pain in her head more severe; her thoughts began to wander, she forgot where she was, everything became confused, and at length she lost all consciousness.

Several gentlemen, among whom were Mr. Horace Dinsmore and Mr. Travilla, were conversing together on the portico, when they were suddenly startled by a sound as of something falling.

Travilla, who was nearest the door, rushed into the drawing room, followed by the others.

"A light! quick, quick, a light!" he cried, raising Elsie's insensible form in his arms, "the child has fainted."

One of the others, instantly snatching a lamp from a distant table, brought it near, and the increased light showed Elsie's little face ghastly as that of a corpse, while a stream of blood was flowing from a wound in the temple, made by striking against some sharp corner of the furniture as she fell.

She was a pitiable sight indeed, with her fair face, her curls, and her white dress all dabbled in blood.

"Dinsmore, you're a brute!" exclaimed Travilla indignantly, as he placed her gently on a sofa.

Horace made no reply, but, with a face almost as pale as her own, bent over his little daughter in speechless alarm, while one of the

"Dinsmore, you're a brute!" exclaimed
Travilla, as he placed Elsie on a sofa.

guests who happened to be a physician hastily dressed the wound, and then applied restoratives.

At length the soft eyes unclosed, and, gazing with a troubled look into her father's face, bent so anxiously over her, she asked, "Dear papa, are you angry with me?"

"No, darling," he replied in tones made tremulous with emotion, "not at all."

"What was it?" she asked in a bewildered way, "what did I do?—what has happened?"

"Never mind, daughter," he said, "you have been ill; but you are better now, so don't think any more about it."

"She had better be put to bed at once," said the physician.

"There is blood on my dress," cried Elsie in a startled tone; "where did it come from?"

"You fell and hurt your head," replied her father, raising her gently in his arms, "but don't talk any more now."

"Oh! I remember," she moaned, an expression of keen distress coming over her face, "papa——"

"Hush! hush! not a word more! we will let the past go," he said, kissing her lips. "I

shall carry you to your room now and see you
put to bed."

He held her on his knee, her head resting
on his shoulder, while Chloe prepared her for
rest.

"Are you hungry, daughter?" he asked.

"No, papa; I only want to go to sleep."

"There, Aunt Chloe, that will do," he said,
and, raising Elsie in his arms, he carried her
to the bed and was about to place her on it.

"Oh, papa! my prayers first, you know,"
she cried eagerly.

"Never mind them to-night," said he, "you
are not able."

"Please let me, dear papa," she pleaded, "I
cannot go to sleep without."

Yielding to her entreaties, he placed her on
her knees and stood beside her, listening to
her murmured petitions, in which he more
than once heard his own name coupled with a
request that he might be made to love Jesus.

When she had finished, he again raised her
in his arms, kissed her tenderly several times,
and then laid her carefully on the bed, saying,
as he did so, "Why did you ask, Elsie, that I
might love Jesus?"

"Because, papa, I do so want you to love Him; it would make you so happy; and, besides, you cannot go to heaven without it—the Bible says so."

"Does it? And what makes you think I don't love Him?"

"Dear papa, please don't be angry," she pleaded, tearfully, "but you know Jesus says, 'He that keepeth my commandments, he it is that loveth me.'"

He stooped over her. "Good-night, daughter," he said.

"Dear, *dear* papa," she cried, throwing her arm round his neck, and drawing down his face close to hers, "I do love you so very, *very* much!"

"Better than anybody else?" he asked.

"No, papa, I love Jesus best; you next."

He kissed her again, and with a half sigh turned away and left the room. He was not entirely pleased; not quite willing that she should love even her Saviour better than himself.

Elsie was very weary, and was soon asleep. She waked the next morning feeling nearly as well as usual, and after she had had her bath and been dressed by Chloe's careful hands, the curls being arranged to conceal the plaster that covered the wound on her temple, there was nothing in her appearance, except a slight paleness, to remind her friends of the last night's accident.

She was sitting reading her morning chapter when her father came in, and taking a seat by her side, lifted her to his knee, saying, as he caressed her tenderly, "My little daughter is looking pretty well this morning; how does she feel?"

"Quite well, thank you, papa," she replied, looking up into his face with a sweet smile.

He raised the curls to look at the wounded temple; then, as he dropped them again, he said with a shudder, "Elsie, do you know that you were very near being killed last night?"

"No, papa, was I?" she asked.

"Yes; the doctor says if that wound had been made half an inch nearer your eye—I should have been childless."

His voice trembled almost too much for utterance as he finished his sentence, and he strained her to his heart with a deep sigh of thankfulness for her escape.

Elsie was very quiet for some moments, and the little face was almost sad in its deep thoughtfulness.

"What are you thinking of, darling?" he asked.

She raised her eyes to his face and he saw that they were brimful of tears.

"O papa!" she said, "would you have been so very sorry?"

"Sorry, darling! do you not know that you are more precious to me than all my wealth, all my friends and relatives put together? Yes, I would rather part with everything else than lose this one little girl," he said, kissing her again and again.

"Dear, *dear* papa! how glad I am that you love me so much!" she replied; and then relapsed into silence.

He watched her changing countenance for some time, then asked, "What is it, darling?"

"I was just thinking," she said, "whether I was ready to go to heaven, and I believe I was; for I know that I love Jesus; and then I was thinking how glad mamma would have been to see me; don't you think she would, papa?"

"I can't spare you to her yet," he replied
with emotion, "and I think she loves me too
well to wish it."

As Miss Day had not yet returned, Elsie's
time was still pretty much at her own disposal,
excepting when her papa gave her something
to do; so, after breakfast, finding that he was
engaged with someone in the library, she took
her Bible, and seeking out a shady retreat in
the garden, sat down to read.

Presently a servant came to tell Elsie that
her papa wanted her in the drawing room.

She found the company again grouped
about the piano, listening to Adelaide's music.

Elsie went directly to her father and stood
by his side, putting her hand in his with a
gesture of confiding affection.

He smiled down at her and kept fast hold
of it until his sister had risen from the instrument, when putting Elsie in her place, he said,
"Now, my daughter, let us have that song."

"Yes, papa," she replied, beginning the prelude at once, "I will do my very best."

And so she did. The song was both well
played and well sung, and her father looked
proud and happy as the gentlemen expressed

their pleasure and asked for another and another.

Thus the clouds which had so suddenly obscured little Elsie's sky seemed to have vanished as speedily as they had arisen.

Her father again treated her with all his wonted affection, and there even seemed to be a depth of tenderness in his love which it had not known before, for he could not forget how nearly he had lost her.

Chapter 10

In that hour Jesus rejoiced in spirit, and said, I thank thee, O Father, Lord of heaven and earth, that thou hast hid these things from the wise and prudent, and hast revealed them unto babes; even so, Father; for so it seemed good in thy sight.—Luke x. 21

SAYS the Apostle Paul, "I say the truth in Christ, I lie not, my conscience also bearing me witness in the Holy Ghost, that I have great heaviness and continual sorrow in my heart, for I could wish that myself were accursed from Christ, for my brethren, my kinsmen according to the flesh. . . . Brethren, my heart's desire and prayer to God for Israel is, that they might be saved."

And such, dear reader, is, in greater or less degree, the feeling of every renewed heart; loving Jesus, it would fain have others love Him, too; it desires the salvation of all; but for that of its own dear ones it longs and labors and prays. It is like Jacob wrestling with the angel, when he said, "I will not let thee go, except thou bless me."

And thus it was with Elsie. She knew now

that her father was not a Christian; that he
had no real love for Jesus, none of the true
fear of God before his eyes. She saw that if
he permitted her to read to him from God's
word, as he sometimes did, it was not that he
felt any pleasure in listening, but only to
please her; she had no reason to suppose he
ever prayed, and though he went regularly to
church, it was because he considered it proper
and respectable to do so, and not that he cared
to worship God, or to learn His will.

This conviction, which had gradually
dawned upon Elsie, until now it amounted to
certainty, caused her great grief; she shed
many tears over it in secret, and very many
and very earnest were the prayers she offered
up for her dear father's conversion.

She was sitting on his knee one evening in
the drawing room, while he and several other
gentlemen were conversing on the subject of
religion. They were discussing the question
whether or no a change of heart were necessary to salvation.

The general opinion seemed to be that it was
not, and Elsie listened with pain while her
father expressed his decided conviction that

all who led an honest, upright, moral life, and attended to the outward observances of religion, were quite safe.

He could see no necessity for a change of heart; he did not believe in the doctrine of total depravity, not he; no indeed, he thought the world much better than many people would have us believe.

Elsie fixed her eyes on his face with a very mournful gaze while he was speaking, but he was busy with his argument and did not notice her.

But one of the guests was just expressing his approval of Mr. Dinsmore's sentiment, when catching sight of Elsie's face, he stopped, remarking, "Your little girl looks as if she had something to say on the subject; what is it, my dear?"

Elsie blushed, hesitated, and looked at her father.

"Yes, speak, my daughter, if you have anything to say," he said encouragingly.

Elsie lifted her eyes timidly to the gentleman's face as she replied, "I was just thinking, sir, of what our Saviour said to Nicodemus: 'Verily, verily I say unto thee, except

a man be born again, he cannot see the king-
dom of God.' 'Marvel not that I said unto
thee, Ye must be born again.' "

She repeated these words of inspiration
with a deep, earnest solemnity that seemed to
impress every hearer.

For a moment there was a deep hush in the
room.

Then the gentleman asked, "Well, my little
lady, and what is meant by being born again?"

"O sir!" she replied, "surely you know that
it means to have the image of God, lost in
Adam's fall, restored to us; it means what
David asked for when he prayed, 'Create in
me a clean heart, O God, and renew a right
spirit within me.' "

"Where did you learn all this?" he asked,
looking at her with mingled surprise and admiration.

"In the Bible, sir," she modestly replied.

"You seem to have read it to some purpose,"
said he, "and now since you consider that
change so necessary, can you tell me how it is
to be brought about?"

"God's Holy Spirit, alone, can change a
sinner's heart, sir."

"And how am I to secure His aid?" he asked.

Elsie answered with a text: "God is more willing to give His Holy Spirit to them that ask Him, than parents are to give good gifts unto their children."

He paused a moment; then asked, "Have you obtained this new heart, Miss Elsie?"

"I hope I have, sir," she replied.

"Why do you think so?" he asked.

Then raising her eyes to his face, with a touching mixture of deep humility and holy boldness, she continued, "Jesus says, 'Him that cometh unto me, I will in nowise cast him out'; and I believe Him. I did go to Him, and He did not cast me out, but forgave my sins, and taught me to love Him and desire to serve Him all my life."

This conversation between the gentleman and the little girl had drawn the attention of all present; and now Mrs. Dinsmore, who had more than once shown signs of impatience, said, "Well, Elsie, I think you have now talked quite enough for a child of your age." Then, pulling out her watch, "It is high time for little folks to be in bed."

Elsie, blushing deeply, would have retired immediately, but her father held her fast, saying, as he gave his stepmother an angry glance, "You need not go, Elsie, unless you choose; I am quite capable of judging when it is time to send you to bed."

"I would rather go, if you please, papa," whispered Elsie, who had a great dread of Mrs. Dinsmore's anger.

"Very well, then, you may do as you like," he replied, giving her a good-night kiss. And, with a graceful good-night to the company, the little girl left the room.

Her questioner followed her with an admiring glance, then turning to her father, exclaimed warmly, "She is a *remarkably* intelligent child, Dinsmore! one that any father might be proud of."

"Yes," remarked Travilla, "a text has been running in my head ever since you commenced your conversation; something about these things being hid from the wise and prudent, and revealed unto babes. And," he added, "I am sure if ever I saw one who possessed that new nature of which she spoke, it is she herself. Has she any faults, Dinsmore?"

"Very few, *I* think, though she would tell you a different story," replied her father.

The next morning Elsie was sitting reading her Bible, when she suddenly felt a hand laid on her head, and her father's voice said, "Good morning, little daughter."

"Ah! papa, is that you?" she asked, raising her head to give him a smile of joyful welcome. "I did not know you were there."

"Ah! I have been watching you for several minutes," he said. "Always poring over the same book, Elsie; do you never tire of it?"

"No, indeed, papa; it is always new, and I do love it so; it is so very sweet. May I read a little to you?" she added, coaxingly.

"Yes; I love to listen to anything read by my darling," he said, sitting down and taking her on his knee.

She opened at the third chapter of John's Gospel and read it through. At the sixteenth verse, "For God so loved the world, that He gave His only begotten Son, that whosoever believeth in Him should not perish, but have everlasting life," she paused and asked, "Was not that a wonderful gift, papa? and wonderful love that prompted it?"

"Yes," he said absently, stroking her hair.

She finished the chapter, and closing the book, laid her head on his breast, asking, "Dear papa, don't you believe the Bible?"

"Certainly, daughter; I am not an infidel," he replied in a careless tone.

"Well, then, papa," she continued, half hesitatingly, "does not this chapter teach very plainly that we must love Jesus and have new hearts, if we want to go to heaven?"

"Yes," he said, "I dare say it does."

Then taking the book from her, he laid it aside and, giving her a kiss, said, "I was much pleased with your intelligent answers to Mr. Lee last evening."

Elsie sighed, and her eyes filled with tears. It was not what she wanted.

"What an odd child you are!" he said, laughing. "You really look as though I had been scolding, instead of praising you."

She dropped her head on his breast, and burst into tears and sobs.

"Why, Elsie, my own darling, what ails you?" he asked in great surprise.

"Oh, papa!" she sobbed, "I want you to love Jesus."

"Oh; is *that* all?" he said.

And setting her on her feet, he took her by the hand and led her out into the garden, where they met Mr. Travilla and another gentleman, who immediately entered into conversation with Mr. Dinsmore, while Elsie wandered about amongst the flowers and shrubs, gathering a nosegay for her Aunt Adelaide.

Chapter 11

She had waited for their coming,
    She had kiss'd them o'er and o'er—
And they were so fondly treasured
    For the words of love they bore,
Words that whispered in their silence,
    She had listened till his tone
Seemed to linger in the echo
    "Darling, thou art all mine own!"
                        —Mrs. J. C. Neal

"Pray, what weighty matter is troubling your young brain, birdie?" asked Adelaide laughingly, laying her hand on Elsie's shoulder. "One might imagine that the affairs of the nation had been committed to your care."

"O auntie! can't you help me? won't you?" answered the little girl, looking up coaxingly into the bright, cheerful face bent over her.

"Help you in what? reading with your book upside down, eh?" asked Adelaide, pointing with a quizzical look at the volume of fairy tales in her little niece's lap.

"Oh!" cried Elsie, coloring and laughing in her turn, "I was not reading, and did not know that my book was wrong side up. But, Aunt Adelaide, you know Christmas is coming soon, and I want to give papa something, and I am quite puzzled about it. I thought of slippers, but he has a very handsome pair; a purse won't do, either, because I have given him one already, and I would like it to be something worth more than either slippers or purse. But you are so much wiser than I, can't you help me think?"

"Ahem! let me put on my thinking cap," said Adelaide, assuming an air of comic gravity. "Ah! yes, I have it! your miniature, little one, of course; what could please him better?"

"Oh! yes," cried Elsie, clapping her hands, "that will do nicely; why didn't I think of it? Thank you, auntie. But then," she added, her countenance falling, "how can I get it taken without his knowledge? You know the surprise is half the fun."

"Never mind, my dear, I'll find a way to manage that," replied Adelaide confidently, "so just run away with you now, and see how much money you can scrape together to spend on it."

"It won't take long to count it," Elsie said with a merry laugh. "But here is papa just coming in at the door; I hope he won't suspect what we have been talking about," and she bounded away to meet him and claim the kiss he never refused her now.

Once Adelaide would not have been surprised at Elsie's quietness. Patient and sweet-tempered the little girl had always been, but more especially after her father's return from Europe—very quiet and timid, seeming to shrink from observation with a constant dread of incurring reproof or punishment; but the last few happy months, during which her father had continued to lavish upon her every proof of the tenderest affection, had wrought a great change in her. Her manner had lost its timidity, she moved about the house with a light and joyous step, and it was no unusual thing to hear her merry, silvery laugh ring out, or her sweet voice carolling like some wild bird of the wood—the natural outgushings of her joy and thankfulness; for the little heart that had so long been famishing for love, that had often grown so weary and sick in its hungering and thirsting for it, was now fully satisfied and revelled in its happiness.

"I have got it all arranged nicely, Elsie,"

Adelaide said, coming into the room with a very pleased face as the little girl was preparing for bed that evening. "Your papa is going away in a day or two to attend to some business matters connected with your property, and will be absent at least two weeks; so, unless he should take it into his head to carry you along, we can easily manage about the picture."

Elsie looked up with a countenance of blank dismay.

"Why," said Adelaide, laughing, "I thought you'd be delighted with my news, and instead of that, you look as if I had read you your death warrant."

"O Aunt Adelaide! two whole weeks without seeing papa! just think how long."

"Pooh! nonsense, child! it will be gone before you know it. But now tell me, how much money have you?"

"I have saved my allowance for two months, that makes twenty dollars, you know, auntie, and I have a little change besides; do you think it will be enough?"

"Hardly, I'm afraid; but I can lend you some, if necessary."

"Thank you, auntie," Elsie answered gratefully, "you are very kind; but I couldn't take it, because papa has told me expressly that I must never borrow money, nor run into debt in any way."

"Dear me!" exclaimed Adelaide, a little impatiently, "Horace certainly is the most absurdly strict person I ever met with. But never mind, I think we can manage it somehow," she added in a livelier tone, as she stooped to kiss her little niece good-night.

Elsie's gentle rap was heard very early at her papa's door the next morning.

He opened it immediately, and springing into his arms, she asked, almost tearfully, "Are you going away, papa?"

"Yes, darling," he said, caressing her fondly, "I must leave home for a few weeks; and though I at first thought of taking you with me, upon further consideration I have decided that it will be better to leave you here; yet, if you desire it very much, my pet, I will take you along. Shall I?"

"You know I would always rather be with you than anywhere else, papa," she answered, laying her head on his shoulder, "but you know best, and I am quite willing to do whatever you say."

"That is right, daughter; my little Elsie is a good, obedient child," he said, pressing her closer to him.

"When are you going, papa?" she asked, her voice trembling a little.

"To-morrow, directly after dinner."

"So soon," she sighed.

"The sooner I leave you the sooner I shall return, you know, darling," he said, patting her cheek and smiling kindly on her.

"Yes, papa; but two weeks seems such a long, long time."

He smiled. "At your age I suppose it does, but when you are as old as I am, you will think it very short. But, to make it pass more quickly, you may write me a little letter every day, and I will send you one just as often."

"Oh! thank you, papa; that will be so pleasant," she answered with a brightening countenance. "I do so love to get letters, and I would rather have one from you than from anybody else."

"Ah! then I think you ought to be willing to spare me for two weeks. I have been thinking my little girl might perhaps be glad of a little extra pocket money for buying Christmas gifts," he said, taking out his purse. "Would you?"

"Yes, papa; oh! *very* much, indeed."

He laughed at her eager tone, and putting a fifty-dollar note into her hand, asked, "Will that be enough?"

Elsie's eyes opened wide with astonishment. "I never before had half so much as this," she exclaimed. "May I spend it *all*, papa?"

"Provided you don't throw it away," he answered gravely, "but don't forget that I require a strict account of all your expenditure."

"Must I tell you *every* thing I buy?" she asked, her countenance falling considerably.

"Yes, my child, you must; not until after Christmas, however, if you would rather not."

"I will not mind it so much then," she answered, looking quite relieved; "but indeed, papa, it is a great deal of trouble."

"Ah! my little girl must not be lazy," shaking his head gravely.

This was Elsie's first parting from her father since they had learned to know and love each other; and when the time came to say good-bye, she clung to him, and seemed so loath to let him go, that he quite repented of his determination to leave her at home.

"O papa, papa! I cannot bear to have you go and leave me behind," she sobbed. "I feel as if you were never coming back."

"Why, my own darling," he said, kissing her again and again, "why do you talk so? I shall certainly be at home again in a fortnight; but if I had thought you would feel so badly, I would have made arrangements to take you with me. It is too late now, however, and you must let me go, dearest. Be a good girl while I am gone, and when I return I will bring you some handsome presents."

So saying, he embraced her once more, then putting her gently from him, sprang into the carriage and was driven rapidly away.

Elsie stood watching until it was out of sight, and then ran away to her own room to put her arms round her nurse's neck and hide her tears on her bosom.

"Dere, dere, darlin'! dat will do now. Massa Horace he be back 'fore long, and ole Chloe don't like for to see her chile 'stressin' herself so," and the large dusky hand was passed lovingly over the bright curls, and tenderly wiped away the falling tears.

"But, O mammy! I'm afraid he will never come back. I'm afraid the steamboat boiler will burst, or the cars will run off the track, or——"

"Hush, hush, darlin'! dat's wicked; you must jes' trust de Lord to take care of Massa Horace; He's jes' as able to do it one place as in tudder; an' ef you an' your ole mammy keep prayin' for Massa, I'se *sure* he'll come back safe, kase don't you remember what de Good Book says, 'If any two of you agree——' "

"Oh! yes, dear mammy, thank you for remembering it," exclaimed the little girl, lifting her head and smiling through her tears. "I won't cry any more now, but will just try to keep thinking how glad I will be when papa comes home again."

"A very sensible resolution, my dear," said Adelaide, putting her head in at the door, "so come, dry your eyes, and let mammy put on your bonnet and cloak as fast as possible, for I have begged a holiday for you, and am going to carry you off to the city to do some shopping."

"Ah! I think I know what that means, auntie, don't I?" laughed Elsie, as she hastened to obey.

When Elsie laid her head upon her pillow that night she acknowledged to herself that in spite of her father's absence—and she had, at times, missed him sadly—the day had been a very short and pleasant one to her, owing to her Aunt Adelaide's thoughtful kindness in taking her out into new scenes and giving agreeable occupation to her thoughts.

She rose at her usual early hour the next morning, and though feeling lonely, comforted herself with the hope of receiving the promised letter; and her face was full of eager expectation as her grandfather in his usual leisurely manner opened the bag and distributed its contents.

"Two letters for Elsie!" he said in a tone of surprise just as she was beginning to despair of her turn coming at all. "Ah, one is from Horace, I see; and the other from Miss Allison, no doubt."

Elsie could hardly restrain her eagerness while he held them in his hand, examining and commenting upon the address, and postmark.

But at length he tossed them to her, remarking, "There! if you are done your breakfast, you had better run away and read them."

"Oh, thank you, grandpa," she said, gladly availing herself of his permission.

"Elsie is fortunate to-day," observed Lora, looking after her. "I wonder which she will read first."

"Her father's, of course," replied Adelaide. "He is more to her than all the rest of the world put together."

"A matter of small concern to the rest of the world, I opine," remarked Mrs. Dinsmore, dryly.

"Perhaps so, mamma," said Adelaide, quietly, "yet I think there are *some* who prize Elsie's affection."

Yes, Adelaide was right. Miss Rose's letter was neglected and almost forgotten, while Elsie read and reread her papa's with the greatest delight.

It gave an amusing account of the day's journey; but what constituted its chief charm for the little girl was that it was filled with expressions of the tenderest affection for her.

Then came the pleasant task of answering,

which occupied almost all her spare time, for letter writing was to her a rather new and difficult business, Miss Allison having hitherto been her only correspondent. And this was a pleasure which was renewed every day, for her papa faithfully kept his promise, each morning bringing her a letter, until at length one came announcing the speedy return of the writer.

Elsie was almost wild with delight.

"Aunt Adelaide," she cried, running to her to communicate the glad tidings, "papa says he will be here this very afternoon."

"Well, my dear, as we have already attended to all the business that needed to be kept secret from him, I am very glad to hear it, especially for *your* sake," replied Adelaide, looking up for a moment from the book she was reading, and then returning to it again, while her little niece danced out of the room, with her papa's letter still in her hand, and a face beaming with happiness.

As the hour drew near when her father might reasonably be expected, Elsie took her station at one of the drawing-room windows overlooking the avenue, and the moment the carriage appeared in sight, she ran out and waited for him on the steps of the portico.

Mr. Dinsmore put out his head as they drove up the avenue, and the first object that caught his eye was the fairylike form of his little daughter in her blue merino dress, the golden-brown curls waving in the wind. He sprang out and caught her in his arms the instant the carriage stopped.

"My darling, darling child!" he cried, kissing her over and over again and pressing her fondly to his heart, "how glad I am to have you in my arms again!"

"Papa, papa, my own dear, dear papa!" she exclaimed, throwing her arms around his neck, "I'm so happy, now that you have come home safe and well."

"Are you, darling? but I must not keep you out in this wind, for it is quite chilly."

He set her down, and leaving the servant to attend to his baggage, led her into the hall.

"Will you come into the drawing room, papa?" she said, "there is a bright, warm fire there."

"Is there not one in my dressing room?" he asked.

*Elsie ran out and waited for him
on the portico.*

"Yes, papa, a very good one."

"Then we will go there. I dare say the rest of the family are in no great hurry to see me, and I want my little girl to myself for half an hour," he said, leading the way upstairs as he spoke.

They found, as Elsie had reported, a very bright fire in the dressing room. A large easy chair was drawn up near it, and a handsome dressing gown and slippers were placed ready for use; all the work of Elsie's loving little hands.

He saw it all at a glance, and with a pleased smile, stooped and kissed her again, saying, "My dear little daughter is very thoughtful for her papa's comfort."

Then exchanging his warm outdoor apparel and heavy boots for the dressing gown and slippers, he seated himself in the chair and took her on his knee.

"Well, daughter," he said, passing his hand caressingly over her curls, "papa has brought you a present; will you have it now, or shall it be kept for Christmas?"

"Keep it for Christmas, papa," she answered gayly. "Christmas is almost here, and, besides,

I don't want to look at anything but you to-night."

"Very well, look at me as much as you like," was his laughing rejoinder. "And now tell me, have you been a good girl in my absence?"

"As good as I ever am, I believe, papa. I tried very hard; but you can ask Miss Day."

"No; I am entirely satisfied with your report, for I know my little daughter is quite truthful."

Elsie colored with pleasure; then, calling to mind the time when he had for a moment suspected her of falsehood, she heaved a deep sigh, dropping her head upon his breast.

He seemed to understand her thoughts, for, pressing his lips to her forehead, he said, gently and kindly, "I think I shall never again doubt my little daughter's truth."

She looked up with a grateful smile.

"Miss Day has gone away to stay until after New Year's Day, papa," she said, "and so our holidays have begun."

"Ah! I am very well satisfied," said he. "I think you have earned a holiday, and I hope you will enjoy it. But I don't know that I shall let *you* play *all* the time," he added, with a smile, "I have some notion of giving you a lesson now and then, myself."

"Dear papa, how pleasant!" she exclaimed delightedly, "I do so love to say lessons to you."

"Well, then, we will spend an hour together every morning. But are you not to have some company?"

"Oh! yes, papa, quite a houseful," she said with a slight sigh. "The Percys, and the Howards, and all the Carringtons, and some others, too, I believe."

"Why do you sigh, daughter?" he asked, "do you not expect to enjoy their company?"

"Yes, sir, I hope so," she answered, rather dubiously, "but when there are so many, and they stay so long, they are apt to disagree, and that, you know, is not pleasant. I am sure I shall enjoy the hour with you better than any-thing else; it is so sweet to be quite alone with my own darling papa," and the little arm stole softly round his neck again, and the rosy lips touched his cheek.

"Well, when are the little plagues coming?" he asked, returning her caress.

"Some of them to-morrow, papa; no, Mon-day—to-morrow is Sabbath day."

"Shall I bring in de trunks now, Massa?" asked Mr. Dinsmore's servant, putting his head in at the door.

"Yes, John, certainly."

"Why, you brought back a new one, papa, didn't you?" asked Elsie, as John carried in one she was sure she had never seen before, and set it down quite near them.

"Yes, my dear, it is yours. There, John, unlock it," tossing him the key. "And now, daughter, get down and see what you can find in it worth having."

Elsie needed no second bidding, but in an instant was on her knees beside the trunk, eager to examine its contents.

"Take the lid off the bandbox first, and see what is there," said her father.

"O papa, how *very* pretty!" she cried, as she lifted out a beautiful little velvet hat adorned with a couple of ostrich feathers.

"I am very glad it pleases you, my darling," he said, putting it on her head and gazing at her with proud delight in her rare beauty. "There! it fits exactly and is very becoming."

Then taking it off, he returned it to the box and bade her look further.

"I am reserving the present for Christmas," he said in answer to her inquiring look.

Elsie turned to the trunk again.

"Dear papa, how good you are to me!" she said, as she lifted out, one after another, a number of costly toys, which she examined with exclamations of delight, and then several handsome dresses, some of the finest, softest merino, and others of thick, rich silk, all made in fashionable style, and doing credit to his taste and judgment; and lastly a beautiful velvet pelisse, trimmed with costly fur, just the thing to wear with her pretty new hat.

He laughed and patted her cheek.

"We must have these dresses tried on," he said, "at least one of them; for, as they were all cut by the same pattern—one of your old dresses which I took with me—I presume they will all fit alike. Take this one to mammy and tell her to put it on you, and then come back to me."

"Oh! I wondered how you could get them the right size, papa," Elsie answered, as she skipped gayly out of the room.

She was back again in a very few moments, arrayed in the pretty silk he had selected.

"Ah! it seems to be a perfect fit," said he, turning her round and round.

"Mammy must dress you to-morrow in one of these new frocks and your pretty hat and pelisse."

"I am afraid I shall be thinking of them in church, papa, if I wear them then for the first time."

"Pooh! nonsense! what harm if you do? This squeamishness, Elsie, is the one thing about you that displeases me very much. But there! don't look so distressed, my pet. I dare say you will get over it by and by, and be all I wish; indeed, I sometimes think you have improved a little already in that respect."

Oh! what a pang these words sent to her heart! was it indeed true that she was losing her tenderness of conscience? that she was becoming less afraid of displeasing and dishonoring her Saviour than in former days? The very thought was anguish.

Her head drooped and the small white hands were clasped convulsively together, while a silent, earnest prayer for pardon and help went up to Him whose ear is ever open to the cry of His children.

Her father looked at her in astonishment.

"What is it, darling?" he asked, drawing her tenderly toward him, and pushing back the curls from her face.

"O papa! I—I am afraid I don't—love Jesus—as much as I did," she faltered.

"Ah! *that* is it, eh? Well, well, you needn't cry any more. *I* think you are a very good little girl, though rather a silly one, I am afraid, and quite too morbidly conscientious."

He took her on his knee as he spoke, wiped away her tears, and then began talking in a lively strain of something else.

Elsie listened and answered him cheerfully, but all the evening he noticed that whenever she was quiet an unusual expression of sadness would steal over her face.

"What a strange child she is!" he said to himself, as he sat musing over the fire, after sending her to bed. "I cannot understand her; it is very odd how often I wound when I intend to please her."

As for Elsie, she scarcely thought of her new finery, so troubled was her tender conscience, so pained her little heart to think that she had been wandering from her dear Saviour.

But even her father's keen, searching glance, when she came to him in the morning, could discover no trace of sadness in her face; very quiet and sober it was, but entirely peaceful and happy, and so it remained all through the day. Her new clothes did not trouble her; she was hardly conscious of wearing them, and gave her usual attention to the services.

"Where are you going, daughter?" Mr. Dinsmore asked, as Elsie gently withdrew her hand from his on leaving the dining room.

"To my room, papa," she replied.

"Come with me," he said, "I want you."

"What do you want me for, papa?" she asked, as he sat down and took her on his knee.

"What for? why to keep, to love, and to look at," he said, laughing. "I have been away from my little girl so long that now I want her close by my side, or on my knee, all the time. Do you not like to be with me?"

"*Dearly* well, my own darling papa," she answered, flinging her little arms around his neck and laying her head on his breast.

He fondled her and chatted with her for some time; then, still keeping her on his knee, took up a book and began to read.

Elsie saw with pain that it was a novel and longed to beg him to put it away, and spend the precious hours of the holy Sabbath in the study of God's word, or some of the lesser helps to Zion's pilgrims which the saints of our own or other ages have prepared. But she knew that it would be quite out of place for a little child like her to attempt to counsel or reprove her father; and that, tenderly as he loved and cherished her, he would never for one moment allow her to forget their relative positions.

At length she ventured to ask softly, "Papa, may I go to my own room now?"

"What for?" he asked, "are you tired of my company?"

"No, sir, *oh! no;* but I want—" she hesitated and hung her head for an instant, while the rich color mounted to cheek and brow; then, raising it again, she said fearlessly, "I always want to spend a little while with my best Friend on Sabbath afternoon, papa."

He looked puzzled and also somewhat displeased.

"I don't understand you, Elsie," he said, "you surely can have no better friend than your father; and can it be *possible* that you love anyone else better than you love me?"

Again the little arms were round his neck, and hugging him close and closer, she whispered, "It was Jesus I meant, papa; you know He loves me even better than you do, and I must love Him best of all; but there is no one else that I love *half* so much as I love you, my own dear, dear precious father."

"Well, you may go; but only for a little while, mind," he answered, giving her a kiss and setting her down. "Nay," he added hastily, "stay as long as you like; if you feel it a punishment to be kept here with me, I would rather do without you."

"Oh! no, no, papa," she said, "I do so love to be with you. Please don't be angry; please let me come back soon."

"No, darling, I am not angry," he answered, smoothing her hair and smiling kindly on her, "come back just when you like, and the sooner the better."

Elsie did not stay away very long; in less than an hour she returned, bringing her Bible and "Pilgrim's Progress" with her.

Her father welcomed her with a smile, and then turned to his novel again, while she drew a stool to his side, and, sitting down, leaned her head against his knee, and read until the short winter day began to close in, and Mr. Dinsmore, whose hand had been every now and then laid caressingly upon her curls, said, "Put away your book now, daughter; it is growing too dark for you to read without straining your eyes."

Elsie rose at once and without another word laid her books upon the table; then, coming back, claimed her accustomed place upon his knee with her head resting on his shoulder.

He put his arm around her, and they sat silently thus for some moments. At length Elsie asked, "Papa, did you ever read 'Pilgrim's Progress'?"

"Yes; a good while ago, when I was quite a boy."

"And you did not like it, papa?"

"Yes, very much, though I have nearly forgotten the story now. Do *you* like it?"

"Very much, indeed, papa; I think it comes next to the Bible."

"Next to the Bible, eh? well, I believe you are the only little girl of my acquaintance who thinks *that* the most beautiful and interesting book in the world.   But, let me see, what is this 'Pilgrim's Progress' about? some foolish story of a man with a great load on his back, is it not?"

"Foolish! papa; oh! I am sure you don't mean it; you couldn't think it foolish.   Ah! I know by your smile that you are only saying it to tease me.   It is a beautiful story, papa, about Christian; how he lived in the City of Destruction, and had a great burden on his back, which he tried in every way to get rid of, but all in vain, until he came to the Cross; but then it seemed suddenly to loosen of itself, and dropped from his back, and rolled away, and fell into the sepulchre, where it could not be seen any more."

"Well, and is not *that* a foolish story? can you see any sense or meaning in it?" he asked with a slight smile and a keen glance into the eager little face upturned to his.

"Ah! papa, I know what it means," she answered, in a half-sorrowful tone.   "Christian, with the load on his back, is a person who has been convinced of sin by God's Holy Spirit, and feels his sins a heavy burden—too heavy for him to bear; and then he tries to get rid of them by leaving off his wicked ways, and by doing good deeds; but he soon finds he can't get rid of his load that way, for it only grows heavier and heavier, until at last he gives up trying to save himself, and just goes to the cross of Jesus Christ; and the moment he looks to Jesus and trusts in Him, his load of sin is all gone."

Mr. Dinsmore was surprised, as, indeed, he had often been at Elsie's knowledge of spiritual things.

"Who told you all that?" he asked.

"I read it in the Bible, papa; and, besides, I know because I have felt it."

He did not speak again for some moments; and then he said very gravely, "I am afraid you read too many of those dull books. I don't want you to read things that fill you with sad and gloomy thoughts, and make you unhappy. I want my little girl to be merry and happy as the day is long."

"Please don't forbid me to read them, papa," she pleaded with a look of apprehension, "for indeed they don't make me unhappy, and I love them so dearly."

"You need not be alarmed. I shall not do

so unless I see that they do affect your spirits," he answered in a reassuring tone, and
she thanked him with her own bright, sweet
smile.

She was silent for a moment, then asked
suddenly, "Papa, may I say some verses to
you?"

"Some time," he said, "but not now, for
there is the tea bell"; and taking her hand,
he led her down to the dining room.

They went to the drawing room after tea,
but did not stay long. There were no visitors,
and it was very dull and quiet there, no one
seeming inclined for conversation. Old Mr.
Dinsmore sat nodding in his chair, Louise was
drumming on the piano, and the rest were
reading or sitting listlessly, saying nothing,
and Elsie and her papa soon slipped away to
their old seat by his dressing-room fire.

"Sing something for me, my pet, some of
those little hymns I often hear you singing to
yourself," he said, as he took her on his knees;
and Elsie gladly obeyed.

Some of the pieces she sang alone, but in
others which were familiar to him, her father
joined his deep bass notes to her sweet treble,

at which she was greatly delighted. Then they read several chapters of the Bible together, and thus the evening passed so quickly and pleasantly that she was very much surprised when her papa, taking out his watch, told her it was her bedtime.

"O papa! it has been such a nice, *nice* evening!" she said, as she bade him good-night, "so like the dear old times I used to have with Miss Rose, only——"

She paused and colored deeply.

"Only what, darling?" he asked, drawing her caressingly to him.

"Only, papa, if you would pray with me, like she did," she whispered, winding her arms about his neck and hiding her face on his shoulder.

"That I cannot do, my pet; I have never learned how, and so I fear you will have to do all the praying for yourself and me, too," he said with a vain effort to speak lightly, for both heart and conscience were touched.

The only reply was a tightening of the clasp of the little arms about his neck.

Oh! how earnest and importunate were Elsie's pleadings at the throne of grace that

night that her "dear, *dear* papa might soon be
taught to love Jesus, and how to pray to Him."
She rose from her knees feeling a joyful assurance that her petitions had been heard, and
would be granted in God's own good time.

She had hardly laid her head upon her pillow, when her father came in, and saying, "I
have come to sit beside my little girl till she
falls asleep," placed himself in a chair close
by her side, taking her hand in his and holding it, as she loved so to have him do.

"I am *so* glad you have come, papa," she
said, her whole face lighting up with pleased
surprise.

"Are you?" he answered with a smile. "I'm
afraid I am spoiling you; but I can't help it
to-night. I think you forgot your wish to repeat some verses to me?"

"Oh! yes, papa!" she said, "but may I say
them now?"

He nodded assent, and she went on. "They
are some Miss Rose sent me in one of her
letters. She cut them out of a newspaper, she
said, and sent them to me because she liked
them; and I, too, think they are very sweet.
The piece is headed 'The Pilgrim's Wants':

"I want a sweet sense of Thy pardoning love,
    That my manifold sins are forgiven;
That Christ as my Advocate, pleadeth above,
    That my name is recorded in heaven.

"I want every moment to feel
    That Thy Spirit resides in my heart—
That His power is present to cleanse and to heal,
    And newness of life to impart.

"I want—oh! I want to attain
    Some likeness, my Saviour, to Thee!
That longed-for resemblance once more to regain,
    Thy comeliness put upon me.

"I want to be marked for Thine own—
    Thy seal on my forehead to wear;
To receive that new name on the mystic white stone
    Which none but Thyself can declare."

He was silent for a moment after she had repeated the last verse; then laying his hand softly on her head and looking searchingly into her eyes, he asked, "And does my little one really wish all that those words express?"

"Yes, papa, for myself and for you, too," she answered. "O papa! I do want to be all that Jesus would have me! just like Him; so like Him that everybody who knows me will see the likeness and know that I belong to Him."

"Nay; you belong to me," he said, leaning over her and patting her cheek. "Hush! I will have no gainsaying of my words," he added with a mixture of authority and playfulness, as she seemed about to reply. "Now shut your eyes and go to sleep; I will have no more talking to-night."

She obeyed at once; the white lids gently closed over the sweet eyes, the long, dark lashes rested quietly on the fair, round cheek, and soon her soft, regular breathing told that she had passed into the land of dreams.

Her father sat, still holding the little hand, and still gazing tenderly upon the sweet young face, till, something in its expression reminding him of words she had just repeated,

"I want to be marked for Thine own—
Thy seal on my forehead to wear,"

"Ah, my darling, *that* prayer is granted already!" he murmured, "for you seem almost too good and pure for earth. But oh, God forbid that you should be taken from me to that place where I can see that your heart is even now. How desolate should I be!" and he turned away with a shiver and a heavy sigh and hastily quitted the room.

Chapter 12

An angel face! its sunny wealth of hair,
In radiant ripples bathed the graceful throat
And dimpled shoulders.

—MRS. OSGOOD

THE cold gray light of a winter morning was stealing in through the half-closed blinds as Elsie awoke and started up in bed with the thought that this was the day on which several of her young guests were expected, and that her papa had promised her a walk with him before breakfast, if she were ready in time.

Aunt Chloe had already risen, and a bright fire was blazing and crackling on the hearth, which she was carefully sweeping up.

"Good morning, mammy," said the little girl. "Are you ready to dress me now?"

"What, you 'wake, darlin'?" cried the fond old creature, turning quickly round at the sound of her nursling's voice. "Better lie still, honey, till de room gets warm."

"I'll wait a little while, mammy," Elsie said, lying down again, "but I must get up soon; for I wouldn't miss my walk with papa for a great deal. Please throw the shutters wide open and let the daylight in. I'm so glad it has come."

"Why, my bressed lamb, you didn't lie awake lookin' for de mornin', did you? You ain't sick, nor sufferin' any way?" exclaimed Chloe in a tone of mingled concern and inquiry, as she hastily set down her broom and came toward the bed.

"Oh, no, mammy! I slept nicely and feel as well as can be," replied the little girl, "but I am glad to see this new day, because I hope it is going to be a very happy one. Carry Howard and a good many of my little friends are coming, you know, and I think we will have a very pleasant time together."

"Your ole mammy hopes you will, darlin'," replied Chloe heartily, "an' I'se glad 'nough to see you lookin' so bright an' well; but jes' you lie still till it gets warm here. I'll open de shutters an' fotch some more wood for de fire an' clar up de room, an' by dat time I reckon you can get up."

Elsie waited patiently till Chloe pronounced the room warm enough, then sprang up with an eager haste, asking to be dressed as quickly as possible, that she might go to her papa.

"Don't you go for to worry yourself, dar-lin'; dere's plenty ob time," said Chloe, begin-ning her work with all speed, however, "de mistress has ordered de breakfast at nine, dese holiday times, to let de ladies an' gen'lemen take a mornin' nap if dey likes it."

"Oh, yes, mammy! and that reminds me that papa said I must eat a cracker or something before I take my walk, because he thinks it isn't good for people to exercise much on an entirely empty stomach," said Elsie. "Will you get me one when you have done my curls?"

"Yes, honey; dere's a paper full in de drawer yonder," replied Chloe, "an' I reckon you better eat two or three, or you'll be mighty hungry 'fore you gits your breakfast."

It still wanted a few minutes of eight o'clock when Elsie's gentle rap was heard at her papa's dressing-room door. He opened it, and stoop-ing to give her a good-morning kiss, said, "How bright and well my darling looks! Had you a good night's rest?"

"Oh, yes, papa! I never waked once till it began to be light," she replied, "and now I'm all ready for our walk."

"In good season, too," he said. "Well, we

will start presently; but take off your hat and
come and sit on my knee a little while first;
breakfast will be late this morning, and we
need not hurry.   Did you get something to
eat?" he asked, as he seated himself by the
fire and drew her to his side.

"Yes, papa, I ate a cracker, and I think I
will not get very hungry before nine o'clock;
and I'm very glad we have so much time for
our walk," she replied, as she took her place
on his knee.   "Shall we not start soon?"

"Presently," he said, stroking her hair; "but
it will not hurt you to get well warmed first,
for it is a sharp morning."

"You are very careful of me, dear papa,"
she said, laying her head on his breast, "and
oh! it is so nice to have a papa to love me and
take care of me."

"And it is so nice to have a dear little daughter to love and to take care of," he answered,
pressing her closer to him.

The house was still very quiet, no one seeming to be astir but the servants, as Mr. Dinsmore and Elsie went down the stairs and
passed out through the hall.

Breakfast—always a plentiful and inviting

meal at Roselands—was already upon the table when they returned, and they brought to it appetites sufficiently keen to make it very enjoyable.

Elsie spent the first hour after breakfast at the piano, practicing, and the second in her papa's dressing room, studying and reciting to him; then they took a long ride on horseback, and when they returned she found that quite a number of the expected guests had already arrived.

Among them was Caroline Howard, a favorite friend of Elsie's; a pretty, sweet-tempered little girl about a year older than herself.

Caroline had been away paying a long visit to some friends in the North, and so the two little girls had not met for nearly a year, and of course they had a great deal to say to each other.

They chatted a few moments in the drawing room, and then Elsie carried her friend off with her to her own room, that they might go on with their talk while she was getting dressed for dinner. Caroline had much to tell of her Northern relatives, and of all she had seen and heard, and Elsie of her new-found parent and her happiness in being so loved and cared for; and so the little tongues ran very fast, neither of them feeling Chloe's presence any restraint. But she soon completed her task, and went out, leaving the two sitting on the sofa together, laughing and talking merrily while awaiting the summons to dinner, which they were to take that day along with their elders.

"How pretty your hair is, Elsie," said Caroline, winding the glossy ringlets around her finger, "I wish you'd give me one of these curls. I want to get a bracelet made for mamma, and she thinks so much of you, and your hair is such a lovely color, that I am sure she would be delighted with one made of it."

"A Christmas gift is it to be?" asked Elsie, "but how will you get it done in time? for you know day after to-morrow is Christmas."

"Yes, I know, but if I could get into the city this afternoon, I think I might get them to promise it by to-morrow night."

"Well, you shall have the curl, at any rate, if you will just take the scissors and help yourself, and poor mammy will have the fewer to curl the next time," Elsie answered, laughingly. "But mind that you take it where it will not be missed."

"Of course I will; I don't want to spoil your beauty, though you are so much prettier than I," was Caroline's laughing rejoinder. "There," she cried, holding up the severed ringlet, "isn't it a beauty? But don't look scared; it will never be missed among so many."

"Well," Elsie said, shaking back her curls, "suppose we go down to the drawing room now, and I will ask papa to take us to the city this afternoon; or, if he is too busy to go himself, to let Pomp or Ajax drive us in."

"I think it would be better fun to go alone, Elsie—don't you?" asked Caroline with some hesitation, adding quickly: "Don't be vexed, but I must confess I am more than half afraid of your father."

"Oh! you wouldn't be, Carry, if you knew him," Elsie answered, in her eager way.

They found Mr. Dinsmore in the drawing room, where most of the guests and the older members of the family were assembled. He was conversing with a strange gentleman. She had to wait some moments, for the gentle-

"*Mind you take it where it will not be
missed,*" said Elsie, laughing.

men were discussing some political question and were too much engaged to notice her.

But at length her father put his arm around her and with a kind smile asked, "What is it, daughter?"

"Carry and I want to go to the city this afternoon; won't you take us, papa?"

"I wish I could, my dear, but I have an engagement which makes it quite impossible."

"Ah, I'm so sorry; but then, papa, we may have one of the carriages, and Pomp or Ajax to drive us, may we not?"

"No, daughter, I am sorry to disappoint you, but I am afraid you are too young to be trusted on such an expedition with only a servant. You must wait until to-morrow, when I can take you myself."

"But, papa, we want to go to-day. Oh! please do say yes; we want to go so very much, and I'm sure we could do very nicely by ourselves."

Her arm was around his neck, and both tone and look were very coaxing.

"My little daughter forgets that when papa says no, she is never to ask again."

Elsie blushed and hung her head. His manner was quite too grave and decided for her to venture another word.

"What is the matter? what does Elsie want?" asked Adelaide, who was standing near and had overheard enough to have some idea of the trouble.

Mr. Dinsmore explained, and Adelaide at once offered to take charge of the little girls, saying that she intended shopping a little in the city herself that very afternoon.

"Thank you," said her brother, looking very much pleased, "that obviates the difficulty entirely. Elsie, you may go, if Mrs. Howard gives Caroline permission."

"Thank you, dear papa, thank you so very much," she answered gratefully, and then ran away to tell Carry of her success, and secure Mrs. Howard's permission, which was easily obtained.

Elsie had intended buying some little present for each of the house-servants, and had taken a great deal of pleasure in making out a list of such articles as she thought would be suitable; but, on examining her purse, she found to her dismay that she had already spent so much on the miniature, and various gifts in-

tended for other members of the family, that
there was very little left; and it was with a
very sober, almost sorrowful face, that she
came down to take her place in the carriage;
it brightened instantly, though, as she caught
sight of her father waiting to see her off.

"All ready, my darling?" he said, holding
out his hand. "I think you will have a pleasant ride."

"Ah! yes, if you were only going too, papa,"
she answered regretfully.

"Quite impossible, my pet; but here is something to help you in your shopping; use it
wisely"; and he put a twenty-dollar gold piece
in her hand.

"Oh, thank you, papa! how good and kind
you are to me!" she exclaimed, her whole face
lighting up with pleasure, "now I can buy
some things I wanted to get for mammy and
the rest. But how could you know I wanted
more money?"

He only smiled, lifted her up in his arms
and kissed her fondly; then, placing her in
the carriage, said to the coachman, "Drive
carefully, Ajax; you are carrying my greatest
treasure."

"Nebber fear, marster; dese ole horses nebber tink of running away," replied the negro with a bow and a grin, as he touched his horses with the whip and drove off.

It was growing quite dark when the carriage again drove up the avenue; and Mr. Horace Dinsmore, who was beginning to feel a little anxious, came out to receive them and asked what had detained them so long.

"Long!" said Adelaide in a tone of surprise, "you gentlemen really have no idea what an undertaking it is to shop. Why, I thought we got through in a wonderfully short time."

"O papa, I have bought such quantities of nice things," cried Elsie.

"Such as tobacco, pipes, red flannel, et cetera," remarked Adelaide, laughing.

"Indeed, Miss Adelaide!" exclaimed Carry, somewhat indignantly, "you forget the——"

But Elsie's little hand was suddenly placed over her mouth, and Carry laughed pleasantly, saying, "Ah! I forgot, I mustn't tell."

"Papa, papa," cried Elsie, catching hold of his hand, "do come with me to my room, and let me show you my purchases."

"I will, darling," he answered, pinching her cheek. "Here, Bill"—to a servant—"carry these bundles to Miss Elsie's room."

Then, picking her up, he tossed her over his shoulder and carried her upstairs, as easily as though she had been a baby, she clinging to him and laughing merrily.

"Why, papa, how strong you are," she said, as he set her down. "I believe you can carry me as easily as I can my doll."

"To be sure; you are my doll," said he, "and a very light burden for a man of my size and strength. But here come the bundles! what a number! no wonder you were late in getting home."

"Oh! yes, papa, see! I want to show you!" and catching up one of them, she hastily tore it open, displaying a very gay handkerchief. "This is a turban for Aunt Phillis; and this is a pound of tobacco for old Uncle Jack, and a nice pipe, too. Look, mammy! won't he be pleased? And here's some flannel for poor old Aunt Dinah, who has the rheumatism; and that—oh! no, no, mammy! don't you open that! It's a nice shawl for her, papa," she whispered in his ear.

"Ah!" he said, smiling, "and which is my present? You had better point it out, lest I should stumble upon it and learn the secret too soon."

"There is none here for you, sir," she replied, looking up into his face with a smile. "I would give you the bundle you carried upstairs just now, but I'm afraid you would say that was not mine to give, because it belongs to you already."

"Indeed it does, and I feel richer in that possession than all the gold of California could make me," he said, pressing her to his heart.

"My own papa! I'm so glad I do belong to you," she said, throwing her arms around his neck and laying her cheek to his for an instant. Then springing away, she added, "But I must show you the rest of the things."

And she went on opening bundle after bundle, displaying their contents and telling him for whom she intended them, until at last they had all been examined, and then she said, a little wearily, "Now, mammy, please put them all away until to-morrow. But first take off my things and get me ready to go downstairs."

"No, daughter," Mr. Dinsmore said in a gentle but firm tone, "you are not ready to have them put away until the price of each has been set down in your book."

Elsie's face clouded, and the slightest approach to a pout might have been perceived.

"I hope my little girl is not going to be naughty," he said, very gravely.

Her face brightened in an instant. "No, papa," she answered cheerfully, "I will be good and do whatever you bid me."

"That is my own darling," said he, "and I will help you, and it will not take long."

He opened her writing desk as he spoke and took out her account book.

"Oh! papa!" she cried in a startled tone, springing forward and taking hold of his hand, "please, please don't look! you know you said I need not show you until after Christmas."

"No, I will not," he replied, smiling at her eagerness, "you shall put down the items in the book, while I write the labels and Aunt Chloe pins them on. Will that do?"

"Oh! that's a nice plan, papa," she said gayly, as she threw off her hat and pelisse, and, seating herself before the desk, took out her pen and ink.

Half an hour's work finished it all, and Elsie wiped her pen and laid it away, saying joyously, "Oh! I'm so glad it is all done."

"Papa knew best, after all, did he not?" asked her father.

"Yes, papa," she said softly, "you always know best, and I am very sorry I was naughty."

He answered with a kiss, and, taking her hand, led her down to the drawing room.

After tea the young people adjourned to the nursery, where they amused themselves with a variety of innocent games. Quite early in the evening, and greatly to Elsie's delight, her father joined them; and, though some of the young strangers were at first rather shy of him, they soon found that he could enter heartily into their sports, and before the time came to separate for the night, he had made himself very popular with nearly all.

Time flew fast, and Elsie was very much surprised when the clock struck eight. Half-past was her bedtime, and she thought the hands had never moved so fast. As it struck the half hour she drew near her father's side.

"Papa," she asked, "is the clock right?"

"Yes, my dear, it is," he replied, comparing it with his watch.

"And must I go to bed now?" she asked, half hoping for permission to stay up a little longer.

"Yes, daughter; keep to rules."

Elsie looked disappointed, and several little voices urged, "Oh, do let her stay up another hour, or at least till nine o'clock."

"No; I cannot often allow a departure from rules," he said kindly, but firmly, "and to-morrow night Elsie will find it harder to go to bed in season than to-night. Bid your little friends good-night, my dear, and go at once."

Elsie obeyed readily and cheerfully. "You, too, papa," she said, coming to him last.

"No, darling," he answered, laying his hand caressingly on her head and smiling approvingly on her, "I will come for my good-night kiss before you are asleep."

Elsie looked very glad and went away feeling herself the happiest little girl in the land, in spite of the annoyance of being forced to leave the merry group in the nursery. She was just ready for bed when her papa came in, and, taking her in his arms, folded her to his heart, saying, "My own darling! my good, obedient little daughter!"

"Dear papa, I love you so much!" she replied, twining her arms around his neck, "I love you all the better for never letting me have my own way, but always making me obey and keep to rules."

"I don't doubt it, daughter," he said, "for I have often noticed that spoiled, petted children usually have very little love for their parents, or indeed for anyone but themselves. But I must put you in your bed, or you will be in danger of taking cold."

He laid her down, tucked the clothes snugly about her, and pressing one more kiss on the round, rosy cheek, left her to her slumbers.

Chapter 13

You play the spaniel,
And think with wagging of your tongue to win me.
—SHAKESPEARE'S *Henry VIII*

These delights, if thou canst give,
Mirth, with thee I mean to live.
—MILTON'S *L'Allegro*

THE young party at Roselands had now grown so large—several additions having been made to it on Monday afternoon and evening—that a separate table was ordered to be spread for them in the nursery, where they took their meals together, Mrs. Brown, the housekeeper, taking the head of the table, for the double purpose of keeping them in order and seeing that their wants were well supplied.

Elsie came in to breakfast from a brisk walk with her papa, looking fresh and rosy, and bright as the morning; quite different from some of the little guests, who had been up far beyond their usual hours the night before, and, having just left their beds, had come down pale and languid in looks, and in some instances showing peevish and fretful tempers, very trying to the patience of their attendants.

"O Elsie!" exclaimed Carry Howard, as the little girl took her place at the table, "we were all so sorry that you had to leave us so soon last night; we had lots of fun after you left. I think your papa might have let you stay up a little longer; but he has promised that to-night—as we are to have the Christmas tree, and ever so much will be going on—you shall stay up till half-past nine, if you like. Won't that be fun? Aren't you glad? I'm sure I am."

"Yes, papa is very kind, and I know I feel much better for going to bed early last night," said Elsie cheerfully.

"Yes, indeed," remarked Mrs. Brown, "late hours and rich food are very bad for little folks, and I notice that Miss Elsie has grown a great deal stronger and healthier-looking since her papa came home; he takes such good care of her."

"Indeed he does," said Elsie heartily, thanking Mrs. Brown with one of her sweetest smiles.

"What are we going to do to-day, Elsie?" asked Caroline.

"Whatever you all prefer," said Elsie. "If you like I will practice that duet with you the first hour after breakfast, or do anything else you wish; but the second hour I must spend with papa, and after that I have nothing to do but entertain my company all day."

"Do you do lessons in holidays?" asked Mary Leslie, a merry, fun-loving child, about Elsie's own age, who considered lessons an intolerable bore, and had some vague idea that they must have been invented for the sole purpose of tormenting children. Her blue eyes opened wide with astonishment when Elsie quietly replied that her papa had kindly arranged to give her an hour every morning, because he knew it would be so much pleasanter for her than spending the whole day in play.

Elsie did keenly enjoy that quiet hour spent in studying and reciting to her father, sitting on a low stool at his feet, or perhaps oftener on his knee with his arm around her waist.

When Elsie left her father she found that the Carringtons had just arrived. She and Lucy had not seen each other since the week the latter had spent at Roselands early in the summer, and both felt pleased to meet.

Several of the older boys had gone out walking or riding, but the younger ones and all the little girls were gathered in a little back parlor, where, by Adelaide's care and forethought, a variety of storybooks, toys, and games had been provided for their amusement. Elsie's entrance was hailed with delight, for she was a general favorite.

"Oh! Elsie, can't you tell us what to play?" cried Mary Leslie.

Elsie proposed that they should all take a walk as the day was fine, and there would be plenty of time before dinner.

The motion was carried without a dissenting voice, and in a few moments they all set out, a very merry party, full of fun and frolic. They had a very pleasant time and returned barely in season to be dressed for dinner.

They dined by themselves in the nursery, but were afterward taken down to the drawing room. Here Elsie found herself immediately seized upon by a young lady dressed in very gay and fashionable style, whom she did not remember ever to have seen before, but who insisted on seating the little girl on the sofa by her side and keeping her there a long while, loading her with caresses and flattery.

"My dear child," she said, "what lovely hair you have! so fine, and soft, and glossy; such a beautiful color, too, and curls so *splendidly! Natural* ringlets, I'm sure, are they not?"

"Yes, ma'am," Elsie answered simply, wishing from the bottom of her heart that the lady would release her and talk to someone else.

But the lady had no such intention.

"You are a very sweet little girl, I am sure, and I shall love you dearly," she said, kissing her several times. "Ah! I would give *anything* if I had such a clear, fair complexion and such rosy cheeks. That makes you blush. Well, I like to see it; blushes are very becoming. Oh! you needn't pretend you don't know you're handsome; you're a perfect little beauty. Do tell me, where did you get such splendid eyes? But I needn't ask, for I have only to look at your father to see where they came from. Mr. Dinsmore"—to Elsie's papa, who just then came toward them—"you ought to be very proud of this child; she is the very image of yourself and a perfect little beauty, too."

"Miss Stevens is pleased to flatter me," he said, bowing low, "but flattery is not good for either grown-up children or younger ones, and I must beg leave to decline the compliment, as I cannot see that Elsie bears the slightest resemblance to me or any of my family. She is very like her mother, though," he added, with a half sigh and a tender, loving glance at his little girl, "and that is just what I would have her. But I am forgetting my errand, Miss Stevens; I came to ask if you will ride this afternoon, as we are getting up a small party."

"Yes, thank you, I should like it dearly, it is such a lovely day. But how soon do you start?"

"As soon as the ladies can be ready. The horses will be at the door in a very few moments."

"Ah! then I must go and prepare," she said, rising and sailing out of the room.

Mr. Dinsmore took the seat she had vacated, and, passing his arm round his little girl, said to her in an undertone, "My little daughter must not be so foolish as to believe that people mean all they say to her; for some persons talk in a very thoughtless way, and, without perhaps intending to be exactly untruthful, say a great deal that they really do not mean. And I should be sorry, indeed, to see my little girl so spoiled by all this silly flattery as to grow up conceited and vain."

She looked at him with her own sweet innocent smile, free from the touch of vanity.

"No, papa," she said, "I do not mind when people say such things, because I know the Bible says, 'Favor is deceitful, and Beauty is vain'; and in another place, 'He that flattereth his neighbor spreadeth a net for his feet.' So I will try to keep away from that lady; shall I not, papa?"

"Whenever you can do so without rudeness, daughter," and he moved away, thinking to himself, "How strangely the teachings of that book seem to preserve my child from every evil influence."

A sigh escaped him. There was lurking within his breast a vague consciousness that her father needed such a safeguard, but had it not.

Lucy, who was standing at the window, turned quickly round.

"Come, girls," she said, "let us run out and see them off; they're bringing up the horses. And see, there's Miss Adelaide in her riding-dress and cap; how pretty she looks! And there's that Miss Stevens coming out now; hateful thing! I can't bear her! Come, Elsie and Carry!"

And she ran out, Caroline and Elsie following. Elsie, however, went no further than the hall, where she stood still at the foot of the stairs.

"Come, Elsie," called the other two from the portico, "come out here."

"No," replied the little girl, "I cannot come without something round me. Papa says it is too cold for me to be out in the wind to-day with my neck and arms bare."

"Pooh! nonsense!" said Lucy, " 'tain't a bit cold; *do* come now."

"No, Lucy, I must obey my father," Elsie answered in a very pleasant but no less decided tone.

Someone caught her round the waist and lifted her up.

"Oh! papa," she exclaimed, "I did not know you were there! I wish I was going too; I don't like to have *you* go without me."

"I wish you were, my pet; I always love to have you with me; but you know it wouldn't do; you have your little guests to entertain. Good-bye, darling. Don't go out in the cold."

He kissed her, as he always did now, when leaving her even for an hour or two, and set her down.

The little girls watched until the last of the party had disappeared down the avenue, and then ran gayly upstairs to Elsie's room, where they busied themselves until teatime in various little preparations for the evening, such as dressing dolls, and tying up bundles of candy, to be hung upon the Christmas tree.

The children had all noticed that the doors of a parlor opening into the drawing room had been closed since morning to all but a favored few, who passed in and out with an air of mystery and importance, and generally laden with some odd-looking bundle when going in, which they invariably left behind on coming out again, and many a whispered consultation

*They busied themselves tying up bundles
to be hung on the Christmas tree.*

had been held as to what was probably going on in there. Elsie and Carry seemed to be in the secret, but only smiled and shook their heads wisely when questioned.

But at length tea being over, and all, both old and young, assembled as if by common consent in the drawing room, it began to be whispered about that their curiosity was now on the point of being gratified.

All were immediately on the *qui vive,* and every face brightened with mirth and expectation; and when, a moment after, the doors were thrown open, there was a universal burst of applause.

A large Christmas tree had been set up at the further end of the room, and, with its myriad of lighted tapers and its load of toys and bonbons interspersed with many a richer and more costly gift, made quite a display.

"Beautiful! beautiful!" cried the children, clapping their hands and dancing about with delight, while their elders, perhaps equally pleased, expressed their admiration after a more staid and sober fashion. When they thought their handiwork had been sufficiently admired, Mrs. Dinsmore and Adelaide ap-

proached the tree and began the pleasant task
of distributing the gifts.

Everything was labeled, and each, as his or
her name was called out, stepped forward to
receive the present.

No one had been forgotten; each had something, and almost everyone had several pretty
presents. Mary Leslie and little Flora Arndt
were made perfectly happy with wax dolls that
could open and shut their eyes; Caroline Howard received a gold chain from her mamma
and a pretty pin from Elsie; Lucy, a set of
coral ornaments, besides several smaller presents; and others were equally fortunate. All
was mirth and hilarity; only one clouded face
to be seen, and that belonged to Enna, who was
pouting in a corner because Mary Leslie's doll
was a little larger than hers.

Elsie had already received a pretty bracelet from her Aunt Adelaide, a needlecase from
Lora, and several little gifts from her young
guests, and was just beginning to wonder what
had become of her papa's promised present,
when she heard her name again, and Adelaide,
turning to her with a pleased look, slipped a
most beautiful diamond ring on her finger.

"From your papa," she said. "Go and thank him; it is well worth it."

Elsie sought him out where he stood alone in a corner, an amused spectator of the merry scene.

"See, papa," she said, holding up her hand. "I think it very beautiful; thank you, dear papa, thank you very much."

"Does it please you, my darling?" he asked, stooping to press a kiss on the little upturned face, so bright and happy.

"Yes, papa, I think it is lovely! the very prettiest ring I ever saw."

"Yet I think there is something else you would have liked better, is there not?" he asked, looking searchingly into her face.

"Dear papa, I like it *very* much; I would rather have it than anything else on the tree."

"Still you have not answered my question," he said with a smile, as he sat down and drew her to his side, adding in a playful tone, "Come, I am not going to put up with any evasion; tell me truly if you would have preferred something else, and if so, what it is."

Elsie blushed and looked down; then raising her eyes and seeing with what a tender, loving glance he was regarding her, she took courage to say, "Yes, papa, there is *one* thing I would have liked better, and that is your miniature."

To her surprise he looked highly pleased at her reply, and giving her another kiss, said, "Well, darling, some day you shall have it."

"Mr. Horace Dinsmore," called Adelaide, taking some small, glittering object from the tree.

"Another present for me?" he asked, as Walter came running with it.

He had already received several, from his father and sisters, but none had seemed to give him half the pleasure that this did when he saw that it was labeled, "From his little daughter."

It was only a gold pencil. The miniature—with which the artist had succeeded so well that nothing could have been prettier except the original herself—she had reserved to be given in another way.

"Do you like it, papa?" she asked, her face glowing with delight to see how pleased he was.

"Yes, darling, very much; and I shall always think of my little girl when I use it."

"Keep it in your pocket and use it every day, won't you, papa?"

"Yes, my pet, I will; but I thought you said you had no present for me?"

"Oh! no, no, papa; I said there was none for you amongst those bundles. I had bought this, but had given it to Aunt Adelaide to take care of, for fear you might happen to see it."

"Ah! that was it, eh?" and he laughed and stroked her hair.

"Here, Elsie, here is your bundle of candy," said Walter, running up to them again. "Everybody has one, and that is yours, Adelaide says."

He put it in her hand and ran away again. Elsie looked up in her father's face inquiringly.

"No, darling," he said, taking the paper from her hand and examining its contents, "not to-night; to-morrow after breakfast you may eat the cream candy and the rock but none of the others; they are colored and very unwholesome."

"Won't *you* eat some, papa?" she asked with winning sweetness.

"No, dearest," he said, "for though I, too,

am fond of sweet things, I will not eat them while I refuse them to you."

"Do, papa," she urged, "it would give me pleasure to see you enjoying it."

"No, darling, *I* will wait until to-morrow, too."

"Please keep it for me until to-morrow, papa, will you?"

"Yes," he said, putting it in his pocket; and then, as the gifts had all been distributed, and the little folks were in high glee, a variety of sports were commenced by them, in which some of their elders also took a part; and thus the hours sped away so rapidly that Elsie was very much surprised when her father called her to go to bed.

"Is it half-past nine already, papa?" she asked.

"It is ten, my dear child, and high time you were in bed," he said, smiling at her look of astonishment. "I hope you have enjoyed yourself."

"Oh! so much, papa. Good-night, and thank you for letting me stay up so long."

Chapter 14

Ask me not why I should love her—
Look upon those soulful eyes!
Look while mirth or feeling moves her,
And see there how sweetly rise
Thoughts gay and gentle from a breast
Which is of innocence the nest—
Which, though each joy were from it shred,
By truth would still be tenanted!

—HOFFMAN'S *Poems*

IT WAS yet dark when Elsie awoke, but, hearing the clock strike five, she knew it was morning. She lay still a little while, and then, slipping softly out of bed, put her feet into her slippers, threw her warm dressing gown around her, and feeling for a little package she had left on her toilet table, she secured it and stole noiselessly from the room.

All was darkness and silence in the house, but she had no thought of fear; and, gliding gently down the hall to her papa's door, she turned the handle very cautiously, when, to her great delight, she found it had been left unfastened and yielded readily to her touch.

She entered as quietly as a little mouse, listened for a moment until satisfied from his breathing that her father was still sound asleep, then, stepping softly across the room, she laid her package down where he could not fail to see it as soon as daylight came and his eyes were opened. This accomplished, she stole back again as noiselessly as she had come.

"Who dat?" demanded Chloe, starting up in bed as Elsie re-entered her own apartment.

"It is only I; did I frighten you, mammy?" answered the little girl with a merry laugh.

"Ki! chile, dat *you*? what you doin' runnin' 'bout de house all in de dark, cold night?"

"It isn't night, mammy; I heard it strike five some time ago."

"Well, den, dis chile gwine get right up an' make de fire. But jes' you creep back into de bed, darlin', 'fore you cotch your death ob cold."

"I will, mammy," Elsie said, doing as she was desired, "but please dress me as soon as the room is warm enough, won't you?"

"Yes, darlin', kase ob course I knows you want to be up early o' Christmas mornin'. Ki! Miss Elsie, dat's a beautiful shawl you gave your old mammy. I shan't feel de cold at all dis winter."

"I hope not, mammy; and were Aunt Phillis, and Uncle Jack, and all the rest pleased with their presents?"

"I reckon dey was, darlin', mos' ready to go off de handle 'tirely."

Chloe had soon built up her fire and coaxed it into a bright blaze, and in a few moments more she pronounced the room sufficiently warm for her nursling to get up and be dressed.

Elsie was impatient to go to her father; but even after she had been carefully dressed and all her morning duties attended to, it was still so early that Chloe advised her to wait a little longer, assuring her that it was only a very short time since John had gone in to make his master's fire.

So the little girl sat down and tried to drown her impatience in the pages of a new book— one of her Christmas presents. But Chloe presently stole softly behind her chair, and, holding up high above her head some glittering object attached to a pretty gold chain, let it gradually descend until it rested upon the open book.

Elsie started and jumped up with an exclamation of surprise.

"Wonder if you knows dat gen'leman, darlin'?" laughed Chloe.

"Oh! it is papa," cried the little girl, catching it in her hand, "my own dear, darling papa! oh! how good of him to give it to me!" and she danced about the room in her delight. "It is just himself, so exactly like him! *Isn't* it a good likeness, mammy?" she asked, drawing near the light to examine it more closely. "Dear, dear, *darling* papa!" and she kissed it again and again.

Then, gently drawing her mother's miniature from her bosom, she laid them side by side.

"My papa and mamma; are they not beautiful, mammy? both of them?" she asked, raising her swimming eyes to the dusky face leaning over her and gazing with such mournful fondness at the sweet girlish countenance, so lifelike and beautiful.

"My darling young missus!" murmured the old nurse, "my own precious chile dat dese arms hab carried so many years, dis ole heart like to break wheneber I tinks ob you, an' 'members how your bright young face done gone away forever."

The big tears were rolling fast down the sable cheeks and dropping like rain on Elsie's curls, while the broad bosom heaved with sobs. "But your ole mammy's been good to your little chile dat you lef' behind, darlin', 'deed she has," she went on.

"Yes, mammy, indeed, indeed you have," Elsie said, twining her arms lovingly around her. "But don't let us cry any more, for we know that dear mamma is very happy in heaven and does not wish us to grieve for her now. I shall not show you the picture any more if it makes you cry like that," she added half playfully.

"Not always, chile," Chloe said, wiping away her tears, "but jes' dis here mornin'— Christmas mornin', when she was always so bright and merry. It seems only yesterday she went dancin' about jes' like you."

"Yes, mammy dear, but she is with the angels now—my sweet, pretty mamma!" Elsie whispered softly with another tender, loving look at the picture before she returned it to its accustomed resting place in her bosom.

"And now I must go to papa," she said more cheerfully, "for it is almost breakfast time."

"Is my darling satisfied *now?*" he asked, as she ran into his arms and was folded in a close embrace.

"Yes, papa, indeed I am! thank you a thousand times; it is all I wanted."

"And you have given me the most acceptable present you could have found. It is a most excellent likeness, and I am delighted with it."

"I am so glad, papa, but it was Aunt Adelaide who thought of it."

"Ah! that was very kind of her. But how does my little girl feel this morning after all her dissipation?"

"Oh! very well, thank you, papa."

"You will not want to say any lesson to-day, I suppose?"

"Oh! yes, if you please, papa, and it does not give you too much trouble," she said. "It is the very pleasantest hour in the day, except——"

"Well, except what? Ah, yes, I understand. Well, my pet, it shall be as you wish; but come to me directly after breakfast, as I am going out early."

Elsie had had her hour with her father, but though he had left her and gone out, she still lingered in his dressing room, looking over the next day's lesson. At length, however, she closed the book and left the room, intending to seek her young guests, who were in the lower part of the house.

Miss Stevens's door was open as she passed, and that lady called to her, "Elsie, dear, you sweet little creature, come here and see what I have for you."

Elsie obeyed, though rather reluctantly, and Miss Stevens, bidding her sit down, went to a drawer and took out a large paper of mixed candy, all of the best and most expensive kinds, which she put into the little girl's hands with one of her sweetest smiles.

It was a strong temptation to a child who had a great fondness for such things, but Elsie had prayed from her heart that morning for strength to resist temptation, and it was given her.

"Thank you, ma'am, you are very kind," she said gratefully, "but I cannot take it, because papa does not approve of my eating such things. He gave me a little this morning, but said I must not have any more for a long time."

"Now, that is quite too bad," exclaimed

*"Thank you a thousand times; it is all
I wanted," said Elsie.*

Miss Stevens, "but at least take one or two, child; that much couldn't possibly hurt you, and your papa need never know."

Elsie gave her a look of grieved surprise.

"Oh! could you think I would do that?" she said. "But *God* would know, Miss Stevens; and I should know myself, and how could I ever look my papa in the face again after deceiving him so?"

"Really, my dear, you are making a very serious matter of a mere trifle," laughed the lady; "why, I have deceived my father more than fifty times, and never thought it any harm."

Elsie excused herself and went in search of her young companions.

Miss Stevens had come to Roselands with the fixed determination to lay siege to Mr. Horace Dinsmore's heart, and flattering and petting his little daughter was one of her modes of attack. She had great confidence in the power of her own personal attractions, being really tolerably pretty, and considering herself a great beauty, as well as very highly accomplished.

As Elsie ran out into the hall, she found herself suddenly caught in Mr. Travilla's arms.

"A merry Christmas and a happy New Year, little Elsie," he said, kissing her on both cheeks. "Now I have caught you figuratively and literally, my little lady, so what are you going to give me, eh?"

"Indeed, sir, I think you've helped yourself to the only thing I have to give at present," she answered with a merry silvery laugh.

"Nay, *give* me one, little lady," said he, "one such hug and kiss as I dare say your father gets half a dozen times in a day."

She gave it very heartily.

"Ah! I wish you were ten years older," he said as he set her down.

"If I had been, you wouldn't have got the kiss," she replied, smiling archly.

"Now, it's my turn," he said, taking something from his pocket.

"I expected you'd catch *me,* and so thought it best to come prepared."

He took her hand, as he spoke, and placed a beautiful little gold thimble on her finger. "There, that's to encourage you in industry."

"Thank you, sir; oh! it's a little beauty! I must run and show it to papa. But I must not forget my politeness," she added, hastily throwing open the drawing-room door. "Come in, Mr. Travilla."

There was a large party to dinner that day, and the children came down to the dessert. Miss Stevens, who had contrived to be seated next to Mr. Dinsmore, made an effort, on the entrance of the juveniles, to have Elsie placed on her other side; but Mr. Travilla was too quick for her, and had his young favorite on his knee before she could gain her attention.

The lady was disappointed, and Elsie herself only half satisfied; but the two gentlemen, who thoroughly understood Miss Stevens and saw through all her manoeuvres, exchanged glances of amusement and satisfaction.

After dinner Mr. Travilla invited Elsie, Carry, Lucy, and Mary, to take a ride in his carriage, which invitation was joyfully accepted by all—Mr. Dinsmore giving a ready consent to Elsie's request to be permitted to go.

They had a very merry time, for Mr. Travilla quite laid himself out for their entertainment, and no one knew better than he how to amuse ladies of their age.

It was nearly dark when they returned, and

Elsie went at once to her room to be dressed for the evening. But she found it unoccupied —Aunt Chloe, as it afterward appeared, having gone down to the quarters to carry some of the little girl's gifts to one or two who were too old and feeble to come up to the house to receive them.

Elsie rang the bell, waited a little, and then, feeling impatient to be dressed, ran down to the kitchen to see what had become of her nurse.

A very animated discussion was going on there, just at that moment, between the cook and two or three of her sable companions, and the first words that reached the child's ears, as she stood on the threshold, were, "I tell you, you ole darkie, you donno nuffin' 'bout it! Massa Horace gwine marry *dat* bit ob paint an' finery! no such t'ing! Massa's got more sense."

The words were spoken in a most scornful tone, and Elsie, into whose childish mind the possibility of her father's marrying again had never entered, stood spellbound.

But the conversation went on, the speakers quite unconscious of her vicinity.

It was Pompey's voice that replied:

"Ef Marse Horace don't like her, what for they been gwine ridin' ebery afternoon; will you tell me *dat*, darkies? an' don't dis niggah see him sit beside her mornin', noon, an' night, laughin' an' talkin' at de table an' in de parlor? an' don't she keep a kissin' little Miss Elsie, an' callin' her pretty critter, sweet critter, an' de like?"

"*She* ma to our sweet little Miss Elsie? Bah! I tell you, Pomp, Marse Horace got more sense," returned the cook indignantly.

"Aunt Chloe don't b'lieve no such stuff," put in another voice, "she says Marse Horace *couldn't* put such trash in her sweet young mistis's place."

"Aunt Chloe's a bery fine woman, no doubt," observed Pomp disdainfully, "but I reckon Marse Horace ain't gwine to infide his mater-monical intentions to her; and I consider it quite consequential on Marster's being young and handsome that he will take another wife."

The next speaker said something about his having lived a good while without, and, though Miss Stevens *was* setting her cap, maybe he wouldn't be caught. But Elsie only gathered the sense of it, hardly heard the words, and, bounding away like a frightened deer to her own room, her little heart beating wildly with a confused sense of suffering, she threw herself on the bed. She shed no tears, but there was, oh! such a weight on her heart, such a terrible though vague sense of the instability of all earthly happiness.

There Chloe found her and wondered much what ailed her darling, what made her so silent, and yet so restless, and caused such a deep flush on her cheek. She feared she was feverish, her little hand was so hot and dry; but Elsie insisted that she was quite well, and so Chloe tried to think it was only fatigue.

She would fain have persuaded the little girl to lie still upon her bed and rest and let her tea be brought to her there; but Elsie answered that she would much rather be dressed and join her young companions in the nursery. They, too, wondered what ailed her; she was so very quiet and ate almost nothing at all.

But, indeed, most of the party seemed dull; they had gone through such a round of pleasure and excitement for the last two or three days that now a reaction was beginning, and

they wanted rest, especially the very little
ones, who all retired quite early, when Elsie
and her mates joined their parents in the
drawing room.

Elsie looked eagerly around for her father
the moment she entered the room. He was
beside Miss Stevens, who was at the piano,
performing a very difficult piece of music. He
was leaning over her, turning the leaves and
apparently listening with a great deal of
pleasure, for she was really a fine musician.

Elsie felt sick at heart at the sight—although
a few hours before it would have given her no
concern—and found it very difficult to listen
to and answer the remarks Mrs. Carrington
was making to her about her Christmas presents and the nice ride they had had that afternoon.

Mr. Travilla was watching her; he had
noticed, as soon as she came in, the sad and
troubled look which had come over her face,
and, following the glance of her eyes, he
guessed at the cause.

He knew there was no danger of the trial
that she feared, and would have been glad to
tell her so; but he felt that it was too delicate

a subject for him to venture on; it might seem too much like meddling in Mr. Dinsmore's affairs. But he did the next best thing—got the four little girls into a corner and tried to entertain them with stories and charades.

Elsie seemed interested for a time, but every now and then her eyes would wander to the other side of the room, where her father still stood listening to Miss Stevens's music.

At length Mr. Travilla was called away to give his opinion about some tableaux the young ladies were arranging; and Elsie, knowing it was her usual time for retiring, and not caring to avail herself of her father's permission to stay up until nine o'clock, stole quietly away to her room unobserved by anyone and feeling as if Miss Stevens had already robbed her of her father.

She wiped away a few quiet tears, as she went, and was very silent and sad, while her mammy was preparing her for bed. She hardly knew how to do without her good-night kiss, but feeling as she did, it had seemed quite impossible to ask for it while Miss Stevens was so near him.

When she knelt down to pray, she became

painfully conscious that a feeling of positive
dislike to that lady had been creeping into her
heart, and she asked earnestly to be enabled
to put it away. But she prayed, also, that she
might be spared the trial that she feared, if
God's will were so; and she thought surely it
was, because she had found out that Miss
Stevens was not good, not truthful, or sincere.

"Perhaps dear papa will come to say good-
night before I am asleep," she murmured to
herself as, calmed and soothed by thus casting
her burden on the Lord, she laid her head upon
her pillow.

He, however, had become interested in the
subject of the tableaux, and did not miss his
little girl until the sound of the clock striking
ten reminded him of her, and he looked around
expecting to see her still in the room; but, not
seeing her, he asked Lucy Carrington where
she was.

"Oh!" said Lucy, "she's been gone these
two hours, I should think! I guess she must
have gone to bed."

"Strange that she did not come to bid me
good-night," he exclaimed in a low tone, more
as if thinking aloud than speaking to Lucy.

He hastily left the room. Mr. Travilla followed. "Dinsmore," said he.

Mr. Dinsmore stopped, and Travilla, drawing him to one side, said in an undertone, "I think my little friend is in trouble to-night."

"Ah!" he exclaimed with a startled look, "what can it be? I did not hear of any accident—she has not been hurt? is not sick?—tell me quickly if anything ails my child."

"Nothing, nothing, Dinsmore, only you know servants will talk, and children have ears, and eyes, too, sometimes, and I saw her watching you to-night with a very sad expression."

"Nonsense!" exclaimed Mr. Dinsmore, growing very red and looking extremely vexed, "I wouldn't have had such thoughts put into the child's head for any money. Are you sure of it, Travilla?"

"I am sure she was watching you very closely to-night and looking very miserable."

"Poor darling!" murmured the father. "Thank you, Travilla," shaking his friend heartily by the hand. "Good-night; I shall not be down again if you will be so good as to excuse me to the others."

He went up the stairs almost at a bound, and the next moment was standing beside his sleeping child, looking anxiously down at the little flushed cheeks and tear-swollen eyes, for, disappointed that he did not come to bid her good-night, she had cried herself to sleep.

"Poor darling!" he murmured again, as he stooped over her and kissed away a tear that still trembled on her eyelash.

He longed to tell her that all her fears were groundless, that none other could ever fill her place in his heart, but he did not like to wake her, and so, pressing another light kiss on her cheek, he left her to dream on, unconscious of his visit.